JOLIE

A VALENTINE'S DAY BRIDE

E.E. BURKE

Cover Design by Erin Dameron-Hill

Published by E.E. Burke
eBook ISBN: 978-0-9985382-0-4
Print book ISBN: 978-0-9985382-1-1
www.eeburke.com

CHAPTER 1

February 8, 1877, Noelle, Colorado

*M*en were by nature self-centered, dishonest, unfaithful creatures, and the continued existence *La Maison* only proved this to be true.

The parlor house hadn't been shuttered a week before the men of Noelle were begging the mayor to allow it to reopen, in spite of a vigorous campaign undertaken by a contingent of new brides who'd circulated a petition calling for its permanent closure. The town council had tabled the matter, and when Jolie moved back in and opened for business, they had turned a blind eye.

Men would be men.

"We'll make sure they have no reason to close us down." Jolie hung a sign on the freshly papered wall. *House Rules: No fighting, no swearing, no spitting, no stealing.* "Remind the girls upstairs this goes for them as well as the customers."

The pretty, doe-eyed girl watching Jolie hang the sign nodded. She had an air of innocence about her, which increased her appeal to men, but made guessing her age difficult, especially when she didn't speak.

"I know I don't have to worry about you making trouble," Jolie continued. "Half the time, no one knows you're around."

Angelique glanced in the direction of the stairs leading up to the bedrooms. She communicated well enough when she wanted to.

"Yes, you can go if you'd like. We're done tidying up for now, but be back down here at eight. We have important guests to entertain tonight. Mr. Stiles is bringing along two of the railroad officers who are in town for meetings with the mayor. Reportedly, they like to dance. Wear comfortable shoes. Oh! Before you go up, check in the kitchen with Milly and make sure we have enough bottles of claret and champagne, and the good bourbon whiskey."

When she'd reopened *La Maison*, she'd made a deal with girls: keep the men drinking, so they could keep most of what they earned. Madame Bonheur, their former employer, had taken a hefty cut from what the girls had made, as well as pocketed all the profits from liquor. Jolie had resented her for it, and had sworn she would do things differently if she were ever in charge.

Now, she was in charge. She'd redecorated the house to make it feel more like home to the men who visited. Madame Bonheur had liked to put on airs. Not to mention, she'd broken most of the vases and crystal glassware when she'd gone on a drunken rampage this past Christmas. After trying to shoot the matchmaker, she had spent a week in jail and was only released after promising to leave town.

Good riddance.

A knock sounded on the front door.

"I'll get that," Jolie called out. She paused to check her

hair in the mirror and smoothed down wayward strands. She hated the garish color it had turned after she'd tried to make it golden, and her face was as pale as a corpse. She bit her lips and pinched her cheeks, which didn't really help, then grimaced at her reflection before she turned away. Hopefully, it was no one important. The regulars knew better than to call before noon.

If it did happen to be a customer, she'd call down one of the other girls to entertain him. That was one advantage of being the madam, not having to work upstairs in order to make a living. The worst part of being in the business was putting up with men that were, in a word, repulsive.

Jolie opened the door and sucked in a gasp.

The least repulsive man she'd ever seen stood on the front porch. Arresting blue eyes framed with dark lashes; rich brown hair, clean and shiny and just long enough to tempt a woman's fingers to comb through it; smooth-shaven face with strong lines, yet too classic to be called rugged. He wore a clean, pressed suit—which put him in the minority in the rough mining town—and he held a large case, closed with leather straps. Next to him sat a huge brindle-colored dog.

A smile tugged at Jolie's lips. She hadn't seen a dog that large since she'd bid goodbye to her beloved childhood pet, Soldier. For a heartbeat, she couldn't decide whether it was the man, or the dog, who was a more welcome sight.

"Good afternoon." The man's rich baritone sent shivers down Jolie's spine. His gaze appeared to be trained on a spot a bit to the right, as if he were looking over her shoulder. She glanced back to see if Angelique stood behind her. No, no one else there.

"It's not quite after noon," she pointed out.

"Is this *La Maison*?" He appeared uncertain.

Could he not read the sign? She'd paid dearly to have a new one painted, and had even asked the French-speaking artist to create an image of a *chateau*. The idiot had painted a hat. *Chapeau,* he'd proclaimed proudly. It would've cost too much to repaint it, so maybe that's what had confused the man standing at her door.

"Yes, this is *La Maison*. May I ask your business?"

"Yes, ma'am...or is it Miss?"

"Neither. It's Jolie."

His remarkable blue eyes shifted to her face and narrowed in a way that suggested he was evaluating her features. "As in *très jolie*?"

Ah, a smooth-talker, or he was having a joke at her expense. Either way, she didn't appreciate it. "No, just Jolie."

"Pleased to meet you. I'm Hank Donovan, but just Hank will do. May I come in, Jolie?"

"Yes, of course, *just Hank*."

His lips twisted in amusement. How nice to know he could take a joke, as well as deliver one. Too many men were sadly lacking in humor, and she'd borne the bruises to prove it.

She moved out of the way so Hank could enter. Business was business, after all. She didn't turn down a chance to make money, and neither did the other girls, especially when a customer looked as nice as this one.

"C'mon, Bear. We're going in." He gripped a c-shaped length of rope attached to the dog's collar and the dog preceded him into in the entry, then stopped and waited.

"Bear has better manners than most of our customers," Jolie observed. "And he smells better too. May I pet him?"

Hank reached down to stroke the dog's head. "Let him smell you first."

Jolie offered her hand, which the dog sniffed, then

licked. She gave his master a knowing look. "Gee, I wonder who taught him to flirt?" Crouching down, she rubbed the dog's head and face. "You're a beautiful boy, aren't you?"

"Thank you," Hank replied.

She looked up and arched an eyebrow at him. "I was talking to Bear."

"Oh." Amusement twinkled in Hank's eyes.

Jolie's enjoyment in the moment wavered. His teasing reminded her of the sweet-talking scoundrel who'd lured her away from home, only to betray her. She stood, brushing her hands on her apron to rid them of dog hair. "What can I do for you, Hank?" The man continued to stare at her, which made her feel awkward. Was he scrutinizing her clothing? What did he expect her to be wearing? Obviously, she'd been cleaning. If he didn't like it maybe he should have made an appointment, or at least waited until later in the day to drop by.

"Well?" she asked.

"I've been told this is the best place in town."

"That's true." And she was proud of it. The first madam might've established the house, but Jolie had brought it back from ruin and had made it so much better.

She noticed he hadn't set down the suitcase, which might contain clothing, money, gold dust—who knew what —but she knew why he held onto it so tightly. It wasn't uncommon for men to be relieved of their valuables by unscrupulous women. She ran an honest house though, and the men of Noelle knew that, so she assumed Hank must've recently arrived in town.

All the while, the dog sat patiently waiting, looking up at her with big brown eyes. She reached out to pet him and he pushed his cold nose into her palm.

Hank responded to the tug on the leash by tightening

his grip, but he didn't pull the dog back. He moved closer and his smile broadened, revealing twin dimples. "Bear doesn't usually take to folks quite so fast. You must be special."

She jerked her attention away from the fascinating indentations in his cheeks and took a step backwards. Was he poking fun at her again? Hank was hard to read, and that bothered her. Most of the time, she could size up a man within the first few minutes of meeting him. This one gave off mixed signals—one minute, he was flirtatious, the next polite, but then he seemed almost mean, or was he being sarcastic?

"No, I'm not special, but I do run this house. Do you want a woman?"

"A woman?" His dark brows lifted in a look of surprise, then gathered in confusion, as if he hadn't understood what she asked. He looked around, and an expression flickered across his face that could only be described as embarrassed frustration. Then he recovered the teasing smile. "Does one come with the room?"

Was he trying to be funny? Playing a prank?

"Yes, you get a room with a woman for as long as it takes to finish your business," Jolie responded dryly.

Hank's cheeks colored, her first real hint he wasn't having a laugh at her expense. "This isn't a hotel, I take it."

Oh God. Jolie pursed her lips and fought to restrain a laugh. Was he serious? Well, yes, he must be to look that embarrassed. "Who told you that?"

Hank frowned thoughtfully. "I don't recall their names, but I was told it was by some men at the Golden Nugget."

Jolie harrumphed. Those miners must've thought it would be funny to send Hank and his big dog over here, suspecting Bear would scare the *bejesus* out of her, and everyone would get a big laugh... except for her. And Hank. "Miners can't be trusted."

"So it seems." Hank's smile returned, though this time, it was slightly crooked, which made it all the more alluring. Jolie returned his smile, self-consciously smoothing her hair. Wait, what was she *doing*? A good-looking man crossed her threshold, and she was all but drooling over him. She had better sense than that, she scolded herself, then cleared her throat. "So now that you know it's not a hotel, are you still interested?"

He squinted at her. "Yes, I think I am."

Perhaps he needed spectacles. That would explain why he'd seemed a little unsure when he stepped inside, and probably why he stared at her so intently. She propped her hands on her hips, back to business. "All right, then all that remains to be discussed is price."

"Ah, well then..." He glanced down at the case, still clutching the handle. "I might have to barter. Until I make my sales, I don't have much in the way of cash money."

"We take gold too." Curious, she eyed the hefty suitcase. "What do you have to offer?"

A slow smile spread across his face. "An item that makes women very happy."

"Do tell," she returned in dry tone.

He lifted the case to his chest. "I should show you. Will you take me to my room?"

Oh, but he was a clever one. That's why he was playing innocent and flashing those dimples; he thought he could lure her into giving away her services for free, then he'd open the suitcase and offer her something worthless, like those fake medicines hawked by the last salesman who'd come through town.

She wasn't falling for that, and she hadn't intended on

going upstairs with him anyway. "Let me call down one of the girls and let them decide if what you have in that case is worth their time."

Disappointment flickered across his features as he lowered the case. For some reason, she longed to smooth the tiny crease between his brows. "No, don't call anyone. I've changed my mind. What I'm interested in bartering for apparently isn't available."

Oh no, that puppy-dog face wasn't working. She wasn't letting a silver-tongued devil talk his way into *her* bed. Just thinking about it made her heart beat faster, which was warning enough.

"How do you know?" She maintained the illusion they were talking about someone other than her. "You haven't even *seen* the girls yet."

Hank gave her a wry smile. "I *can't* see them, so it doesn't really matter."

Jolie responded with halfhearted laugh. "Maybe you should wear your spectacles."

"I've tried spectacles. They don't make any difference."

She stared at him. At first, the remark didn't make much sense, then she realized his gaze had continued to shift slightly off to the side, never truly making contact with her eyes. *Impossible. Could it be...?*

"You...you mean you can't..." she stammered. "Are you *blind?*"

"At the moment, more than I want to admit."

Her heart constricted as his expression turned regretful, and a hot flush rushed into her face. She shouldn't have just blurted that out, but what the hell did he expect?

Then again, what did *she* expect? He'd had no reason to announce on the doorstep that he was blind. He hadn't misled her. She'd assumed he could see...and she had also assumed he was a fraud and a flatterer, and knew she could be just as wrong about that as well.

"C'mon boy." Hank and his dog turned to leave, which shook Jolie out of her shocked state.

She slipped past them and stood in front of the door. "I'm sorry. I didn't realize."

"No need to apologize."

She had an irresistible urge to reach out and trace his kind smile with her fingertips. His honest face and intriguing air of innocence might not be faked either. Hank could be exactly what he appeared to be: charming, witty and, yes, endearing.

Now she could see him so much more clearly, but he still couldn't see her. Ha! Maybe that explained why he hadn't immediately run away. What it didn't explain though, was why she'd caught his interest in the first place. Most likely, he was only interested in one thing. She could give him that, and why not? She owed him a kindness after being so rude. It didn't hurt he had an attractive personality to go along with that handsome face. She just had to remember he was still a man, blind or not, and he'd be no different from all the other men.

Fortunately, she was certain she could perform her job without any emotions becoming involved.

CHAPTER 2

*H*ank's nerves jumped when Jolie's slender fingers closed around his wrist, touching just below where his shirtsleeve had pulled up, where his heartbeat throbbed beneath his skin. "You don't need to leave yet, Hank. If this is what you want, it's available."

Her voice had dropped to a lower register. Soft, sensual...if a voice were silk, that's what it would sound like.

Hank swallowed to clear his throat. He wished he could see the expression on her face, but he couldn't make out more than a blurred outline. Her abrupt change of heart took him by surprise. And that wasn't all that surprised him. He struggled to keep his breathing slow and measured. Already his pulse had sped up like he was a green boy. She must know the effect she was having on him. Soon, it would become more than obvious.

What had changed her mind? Had she suddenly become curious about what he carried in the case?

As she leaned closer, he breathed in an evocative fragrance.

Orange blossoms.

How on earth had she found those up here in the snow?

It's perfume, you idiot.

"Won't you come with me upstairs?" Her voice caressed his ear. "You promised to show me what's in the case."

Ah, so it *was* the case. If she kept breathing into his ear, he'd dump the contents at her feet. He could afford to part with one card, if she was willing to take that in exchange for...for whatever she might do. He had little experience with prostitutes and didn't visit them as a rule, but he hadn't taken Jolie as one, at least not until he'd realized he was standing in a bawdy house. He'd been caught up in their banter, impressed at how quickly she'd taken to Bear, and Bear had warmed up to her. He'd found her charming and fascinating, and wanted to spend time with her, so—

He had the oddest urge to laugh. *He* had propositioned *her,* not the other way around. No one who knew him well would believe it.

Hank tugged Bear's leash. "Let's go with Jolie."

She stepped in front of him, stopping them. "I'm sorry, the dog isn't allowed upstairs."

Her words shook Hank out of his euphoria. Was she luring him into a trap? For all he knew, the woman had a protector lurking somewhere nearby. He'd lost money, his watch, even his clothes to dishonest people who saw him as an easy mark. Before he'd found Bear, he'd been beaten up a few times, robbed, and was lucky he hadn't been killed.

Her shadowy form came closer and he could tell she was looking at him, studying him. "You can trust me, Hank."

Something made him willing, perhaps foolishly so, to let go of Bear's leash. He could make out the blurred shape of a narrow face. Unable to resist, he reached up to touch her. Her skin felt smooth and soft, not loose or pocked. With his fingertips, he traced the delicate shape, trying to envision what she looked like. His mind conjured a pixie, a very *seductive* pixie. The tingling at the base of his spine would soon ignite an aching arousal, and before that happened, he should probably get upstairs.

"Stay, Bear."

The soft thud told him the dog had flopped to the floor. Bear would wait at the base of the stairs, but would come if called.

Hank let Jolie lead him up the stairs. She did a good job of letting him know how high he needed to raise his foot, and how many steps he'd need to take before they reached the top. When they entered her room, the first thing he noticed was a sharp odor. *Carbolic acid?* Some doctors used it on wounds and after surgery to prevent sepsis.

She let go of his arm and took his hat. He could feel the bed against the back of his legs. He froze at the sound of a *click*. She'd gone and locked the door. He couldn't help but think this might've been a big mistake. She could knock him over the head with something heavy before he could call out and steal his cards and his money.

"If you'd like, I'll put the suitcase next to the bed. It'll be right beside you. If you reach down you can feel it."

Had she read his mind, or maybe seen something in the way he reacted which may have given her a clue to his thoughts?

"You don't want to see what's in it first?" he asked.

She put her hands on his shoulders and ran them down his arms, producing a rush of excitement. "Later, you can show me."

Later? What a pleasant surprise, she seemed to be more interested in him than the suitcase. He released it into her custody, hearing a surprised gasp.

"My, this is heavy."

"It's my inventory."

"Are you selling anvils?"

"Not exactly."

She moved to one side of the bed and a thud followed. Then she came right back, close enough he could smell her fragrance over the other less pleasing scent. His heart galloped as she grasped the lapels of his coat and peeled it off. His breathing deepened when she drew down his galluses.

"Here," she murmured, "let's get you comfortable, then I'll wash you off."

Wash him? Ah, the carbolic acid solution. He'd heard of prostitutes using it to prevent becoming diseased. That's why the room reeked of it.

Hank's idyllic bubble burst. His body was still eager enough, but the reminder of the true nature of their relationship extracted all the joy out of the moment. When she began to hurriedly unbutton his trousers, he laid his hand over hers. "What's the hurry?"

"I have important guests this evening, and we have a lot of preparation." Her lips brushed his neck in a way that suggested intimacy, but her explanation made it clear he was just another *guest*, and not an important one.

He cupped his hand behind her head and drew her closer to kiss her.

She turned her face away. "No kissing. That's not part of the service."

Flustered, Hank dropped his arm. She must've figured out by now that he wasn't very experienced at this, unlike her, based on how efficiently she was undressing him. Her voice, on the other hand, made her seem younger. Or had he misjudged that about her too?

"How old are you?"

She dropped his trousers. "You're not supposed to ask."

"But I am asking."

"Twenty-one." She slipped the buttons on his shirt open.

He strained to see her features. Did her eyes flash with interest, seductive intent, weariness, or resignation? She was going through the motions, doing what men expected her to do, something she'd done by rote over and over...His stomach knotted at the thought of how many men she'd undressed.

"So, how many years have you..." He attempted to find a way to phrase the question without being crass. "Been working?"

She dropped the tail of his shirt, which she'd been about to lift over his head, and shifted away from him. "Why do you care?"

Suspicion tinged her voice. He couldn't tell if she doubted his sincerity, or simply thought *no one* cared. Sadness slowed his racing heart.

She couldn't have been much more than a girl when she'd started whoring. His sister might've ended up in a similar situation, if he hadn't stepped in to take care of her after her worthless husband had died.

Hank felt like a hypocrite, worrying about Maggie, while being perfectly willing to take the only thing this young woman believed she had to offer. Shame killed what remained of his desire. He reached down and drew up his trousers, then buttoned them.

Her response, a sigh, was audible. "What are you doing?"

"I'm getting dressed."

"Are you bashful?"

"Not particularly." But let her believe it, if it made her feel better. He fastened the buttons on his shirt. After pulling up his galluses, he felt around behind him on the bed for his coat.

She gave an impatient little sigh. "If you prefer to be dressed while we couple, that's fine with me."

He'd promised her a boon. Even if he hadn't taken what she'd offered, he would honor their deal. "I want to show you something."

"Um...all right."

Hank smiled at her dry response. She imagined he meant some strange perversity, no doubt. He found the suitcase right where she'd said it would be. Her honesty, and her concern he believe in her honesty, touched him.

After lifting the case to the bed, he unbuckled the straps and opened it. Her gasp sounded from his right. She was close enough, if he'd reached out, he could've encircled her waist and pulled her against him.

Instead, he reached for one of the packages of cards his sister had carefully put together, tying them with ribbon. He knew exactly what was packed where, and he selected his favorite: a card featuring a large heart made from paper lace, carefully cut and colored. Maggie had described it to him and had guided his fingers over the intricate design. Beneath the heart in gilded lettering were the words, *My Heart's Desire*. Inside was a verse he had dreamed up, something sufficiently romantic a woman would appreciate.

He held out the card.

"Oh, how *beautiful*." Jolie's voice dropped to a hushed whisper as she took it from him. Her awe and appreciation renewed the happiness he'd felt earlier.

"I'm glad you like it."

"Where did you get these?" In the dim room it was hard to tell, but it seemed Jolie was examining the card.

Hank smiled proudly. "My sister Maggie designs them. Another woman helps her make them, and I sell them."

"I've never seen you selling cards around here."

"I just arrived earlier today."

"From where?"

"The Town of Kansas, or Kansas City, as we prefer to call it."

She leaned over the suitcase. "You came all the way out here to sell cards?"

"Some salesmen haul anvils all over the country."

"True enough," she murmured, sounding amused.

"I did come here to sell cards and hopefully gin up more orders, but I also came out because of the opportunity in silver."

"You're a miner?"

He chuckled. "A *blind* miner? Now that would be a first."

"You're not planning to make a prospector out of Bear, are you?"

Jolie had delightful sense of humor.

"He can't hold a pick and shovel, so I suppose that wouldn't work."

"Then what?"

"I hope to find someone who needs a grubstake, an investor."

"Hmm. If you're wanting to invest in a mine, you should talk to our mayor, Mr. Hardt. He owns the largest silver mine in these parts. He's allowed some of the townsfolk to invest. I heard the Fultons talking about it the last time I visited their store."

Hank closed the suitcase and secured the straps. This might be just the opportunity he was looking for. "Where can I find Mr. Hardt?"

"He has an office downtown. You can't miss it."

"Ah, but I guarantee you, *I* could miss it."

They both laughed.

She walked away, and a moment later, she put his hat in his hand. Maybe she'd decided he had stayed long enough. Then she curled her fingers around the crook of his arm. "I'll show you where it is."

Hank couldn't deny being tempted by the chance to spend time with her. More than her sweet smell intrigued him. However, her earlier comment had made it clear he wasn't her top priority. "Didn't you say you had to prepare for guests?"

"They won't arrive until eight, so I have time. Besides, you gave me a lovely Valentine card. I owe you a fair exchange."

CHAPTER 3

Temperatures outside were still below freezing, but with so many newcomers crowding the street, the roads had been churned into mud. Cold as it was outside, Jolie was glad she'd offered to guide Hank over to Mr. Hardt's office. She was enjoying his company.

She still didn't understand why he'd given her one of his Valentine cards. They were valuable. His *inventory*, he said. He made his living selling them. Why would he give one away for nothing in return? Somehow, she would make it up to him. First, she'd lead him to where he needed to go, so he could get there without landing face down in horse shit.

She sidestepped a steaming pile, still hugging his arm. "Manure to your right."

His boots squished the mud as he moved to the left. He gripped his case with one hand, and with his other hand, held Bear's leash.

"We'll reach the boardwalk soon. The businessmen in town paid for it to go as far as the corner, but not all the way to *La Maison*."

"Inconsiderate of them."

"They don't take into account our needs," she explained matter-of-factly. "For the most part, they ignore our existence, unless they're customers. Actually, the customers ignore us too, if we happen to pass one on the street."

"Does that bother you?"

"Not really," she lied. "It's the way of things."

Hank's dog stopped at the edge of the boardwalk. Hank gave him permission to go on, and he stepped up onto the boards, his toenails tapping. His master followed without missing his footing.

Jolie shook her head, amazed, and peered up at him. "Is that dog *guiding* you?"

Hank responded with a slow smile. "He helps me avoid pitfalls."

"I've never seen the like."

"Bear is special. The teachers at the school for the blind in St. Louis thought I'd lost my mind when I told them what he could do. They said it only works because I have limited vision." He released a soft laugh. "*Limited* is right."

How bad was Hank's condition? He didn't have the blank, unfocused look she'd seen in the eyes of other blind men. "Can you see at all?"

He turned his head at her question and seemed to look at her. "I can see the difference between light and dark, make out shapes and forms, and colors. But everything is blurred. It's like looking through a glass window when rain is pouring down the panes."

What a striking image he'd painted, and heartbreaking. She tried to imagine how frustrating it would be. "I'd go mad."

"No, you'd do what you had to do."

"How do you know?"

"You're a survivor."

He observed a lot without his sight. He was also adept at steering the discussion back to her, which wasn't what she wanted to talk about.

She glanced across the street at an abandoned building where she and the other girls had lived for a short time during the Christmas season. They'd been evicted from *La Maison*, so the newly arrived mail-order brides would have a warm and pleasant place to stay until they were properly wed. Jolie still resented the fact she'd been swept aside like so much garbage.

Hank didn't treat her like she was dirt. Even when he'd put his clothes back on and decided he didn't want to engage in sex, he was nice about it. And he didn't act like he was embarrassed to be seen walking around with her.

Two well-dressed women stood at the front door of the abandoned building and appeared to be unlocking it. Jolie recognized one of them, the preacher's new wife, a crusading do-gooder, but the other lady she didn't know. What were those two doing over there?

When the women glanced over their shoulders, Jolie pasted on a smile and tightened her hold on Hank's arm. *See, you two gawkers? I can get a handsome man too.*

Hank glanced at her questioningly. Then he stumbled.

Jolie caught him by the arm and held him up long enough for him to get his foot in front him and regain his balance. He'd let go of the dog's leash, rather than pull Bear into the mud with him. The big dog circled back, and whined and sniffed, no doubt making sure his master was all right.

"Missed that hole," Hank mumbled. There was no hole. He groped for the dog's leash and she guided his hand to it.

Bear's sad brown eyes seemed to accuse her.

She felt horrid for distracting him, and for such a petty

reason. She'd been parading him around, acting like she owned him. He'd only accepted her help because he needed someone to direct him. He hadn't even been interested enough to finish their business, and he didn't even know what she looked like. How disappointed he would be if he could see her clearly, rather than through a watery curtain.

She would get him safely to his destination, then she would leave him be. Being seen with her wouldn't help him establish a good reputation in town. The sooner she was out of his way, the better.

At the corner, she tightened her grip on his arm and halted. "Let's wait here until we have a clear path to cross the street. There's too much traffic."

Hank waited, apparently willing to take her at her word, but his tight-knuckled grip on Bear's leash implied he'd lost a bit of trust in her. She wanted to kick herself again.

After they'd crossed, she led him into the heart of town. Bear deftly avoided obstacles and cleared a path through the crowd. Even the most hardened miners gave the large dog a wide berth and eyed it as if they expected to be eaten.

"You should see the men jumping to get out of the way," she said in a low voice.

Hank's expression turned wry. "That might be the same fellows who packed me off to *La Maison* to get rid of me. They didn't much care for me having my dog in the saloon."

"Are you kidding? Woody brings in his chickens, and the Thorntons' goose follows them in there. Anyone who has a dog takes it along."

"Are any of the other dogs as big as Bear?"

"Not that I know of." Jolie smiled to herself as she imagined the miners' reactions. "They're a bunch of sissies. Zeke Kinnison used to dress in bearskins and scare the bejesus out of folks until he took a wife. Then he cleaned up and I haven't seen him since. I suspect once the newness wears off, he'll be back."

"He won't if he's happily married."

She huffed in disbelief. "There's no such thing as *that* happily married."

"You only see the ones who aren't."

Was Hank being argumentative because he secretly despised what she did? Maybe he had a double standard too, and she just hadn't picked up on it.

"Cobb's Penn Dry Goods is on your left. You might stop in later and see if Liam Fulton wants to purchase any of those cards. He carries nice things like that. I like shopping there."

"Is that where you get your perfume?"

Jolie looked up sharply. Hank had noticed? "Yes. It's imported." She paid dearly for it, but it was worth every penny.

"I like it."

Her heart swelled at the compliment, but she immediately brushed off the ridiculous sentiment. Really, she was getting all worked up over nothing. So what if he liked an expensive fragrance? Who wouldn't?

"We're passing Sheridan's Hardware now. That's where the miners buy most of their supplies. Next is Mr. Hardt's office." She read the sign on the door: "*Noelle Mining and Smelter*. Mr. Hardt runs it; he's also our mayor, and owns most of the real estate in town—including *La Maison*. He's not uppity like a lot of rich men. Just explain what you want, and ask if he'll let you invest."

Hank's chest expanded as if he'd taken in a deep breath.

"Nervous?"

"Does it show?"

"No, I just guessed." He didn't actually appear all that

nervous; she could just feel it. Odd, she didn't generally pick up on people's emotions, mostly because she didn't care. "You look determined."

"I am." He set down the case that held his cards. "The reason I came out here, is I want to give my sister a better life...or better than what I can provide selling the cards she makes. If I'm able to get in on a venture like this silver mine, it'll change everything."

And it would give him back his pride. That's what he didn't say, although he didn't have to put the sentiment into words for her to understand. She knew all about pride. In her case, having too much of it. She also knew better than to get too interested in Hank Donovan. That wouldn't be good for either of them.

She let go of his arm and took a step back. "You're a good salesman, I'm sure you'll get what you want. Best of luck, and thank you for the card."

"Hey, wait...I'm not saying goodbye yet." He reached out for her, and the gesture tugged at Jolie's heart, as if he'd put a leash on that too.

Alarmed, she stepped backwards. "I am."

Jolie's rapid steps faded. She'd gotten him to his destination, and though they'd been having a pleasant conversation, she just...well, she'd run away. He hadn't really expected her to accompany him inside, so he shouldn't be disappointed, and she *had* told him she was busy, so why should it matter she'd left so abruptly?

When Bear pulled in the direction she'd gone, Hank knelt beside him and stroked the dog's head. "I know you like her, I do too, but we can't go after her. She's got other concerns."

Someone passed behind them on the sidewalk, and their steps slowed, then quickened.

Hank knew people thought he was crazy for talking to Bear, but the dog was his friend. They understood each other.

"I hope Mr. Hardt doesn't mind dogs being in his office as much as those miners did having you in their saloon. You need to be on your best behavior."

Hank stood and groped for the door handle. After he opened it, he heard two distinct voices. Two men. He let Bear enter first so he wouldn't trip over anything. The interior of buildings proved difficult to navigate because the light inside was generally dim.

"Excuse me. I hope I'm not interrupting."

"Hello... *What?*" Several feet away, a dark figure moved, along with the sound of a chair's legs scrapping the floor. "What the devil is *that?*"

"That's a big dog," drawled a second man. Hank located him behind a darker shape, which was probably a desk.

"My dog won't hurt you," Hank said quickly to calm their fears. "Bear helps me get around. My vision isn't so good." He didn't tell people how blind he really was, because it put him at too much of a disadvantage.

"Bear? That's a good name for it," said the first man.

"How can we help you?" asked the second.

Hank couldn't guess which of the two voices came from the man he sought. "I'm looking for Mr. Hardt."

"That'd be me," replied the man with the drawl, the one behind the desk. "This fellow hiding behind his chair is Reverend Chase Hammond."

Was the reverend really hiding behind the chair? Hank

couldn't see well enough to tell. He moved forward and Bear obliged, taking him closer to the two men.

"Reverend Hammond, pleased to make your acquaintance. I'm Hank Donovan."

"Nice to meet you, Mr. Donovan, you and your dog. I was just on my way out." The man's figure moved toward the door. "Charlie, we'll talk later about how to resolve the, um, situation by, uh..."

"Finding someone to take the package off your hands."

"Right. It can't be just anyone. Has to be the right sort. She's...picky."

The door creaked open, then shut on the cryptic conversation, and Hank was left with the man called Charlie. Hank considered himself a fairly good salesman, and as Mr. Hardt didn't appear afraid of his dog, he forged ahead.

"Mr. Hardt, would you have a moment to discuss a matter of financial interest?"

"Sure, sit down."

Hank wondered if he was about to run into the chair. He could make out something in front of him. Yep, it was a chair. He pulled it back to sit, and put the case on the floor. Bear sat beside him.

"You're new here in town, I take it?"

With so many men pouring into the town to look for mining jobs, it was impressive that Hardt would take notice of a new face. "Yes I am."

"Did you happen find a good place to stay?" Something in Hardt's tone implied amusement. Why would he find the subject of lodging funny? Unless...the mayor had observed the scene at the Golden Nugget.

"You were in the saloon earlier?"

"Nah, I just heard about it. Another new arrival told me

some fellow brought a *beastly big dog* into The Golden Nugget and the miners had gotten all worked up. He said you were asking about lodging, and they sent you to *La Maison*. Did Bear scare the girls?"

Hank could see how the incident might be considered funny, in retrospect. "I only met one. Jolie. She and Bear got along famously."

"Doesn't surprise me. She's a tough gal."

Tough wasn't really the word Hank would've used to describe her. Jolie had soft skin and fine bones, a sweet scent and a rapier wit. He couldn't go into how he knew all that, but he could share his positive impression. "She does have mettle and a good sense of humor. She's also considerate. She walked me over here so I could find the place."

"And she didn't charge you anything?"

Maybe the mayor meant it as a joke, or his remark reflected what someone might naturally assume, given Jolie's occupation, but his question rubbed Hank the wrong way.

"Not a penny." Hank didn't mention the deal he'd struck, and he wasn't convinced she'd only done him the favor in exchange for the card. Not to mention, sharing their private conversation would be ungentlemanly.

A chair squeaked, as if Hardt had leaned back. "What brings you to town?"

Relieved they were off the subject of Jolie and back to business, Hank patted his case. "I sell unique and unusual greeting cards. But my long-term plan is to invest in something that has greater potential—a silver mine, for example."

"I see. You want to invest in Noelle Mining?"

Hardt wasn't dull-witted, and Hank knew he must see men every day wanting the same thing.

Hank couldn't immediately come up with good explanation for why he was any different, so he just replied in the affirmative. "That's right."

"Why not take your money and start your own operation?"

Hank presumed the mine owner wasn't being argumentative, just straightforward, someone who would appreciate the unvarnished truth. "I can't see well enough to be a miner. Quite frankly, I wouldn't know how to run an operation like yours. I've heard people who can't do the mining themselves can invest in those who can and reap profits from it. So I've been looking for the right opportunity, and you have a reputation as a fair and honest man."

The figure behind the desk shifted forward. "I'm not looking for more investors at the moment."

"You won't even consider it?"

The sound Hank heard next was the other man drumming his fingers on the desk. Impatient, or not able to be still? Until the man asked him to leave, he'd stay put and attempt to make his case.

"I'd only consider it if you're willing to meet the requirements," Hardt said finally.

Hank almost said *yes* immediately, but then decided he needed to know what he was agreeing to first. "Which are?"

"Investors in Noelle Mining must be upright men, who are married and have settled here."

Hank released a disappointed breath through his lips. He didn't meet any of the requirements, except possibly one, depending on Hardt's definition of *upright*. Nevertheless, the mine owner's tone didn't leave the door open for argument, and what was the point? Hank had no wife, and wasn't anywhere close to finding one.

"Thank you for your time, sir. I know it's valuable, so I won't waste any more of it." Hank stood, picked up his case and pushed back the chair, then grasped Bear's leash.

"Hold on there, Mr. Donovan." The mayor's chair creaked again, and his shadowy form moved, approaching Hank from around the desk. "Tell me the truth. Why did you come here? Do you hope to get rich quick?"

That would be the obvious reason. Every man Hank had talked to in Noelle had jabbered on and on about the riches to be made in silver.

"I can't deny the thought has passed through my mind a time or two. But I'm practical enough to know it's not likely to happen. Right now, the only means I have to support my sister and her children is selling cards." Hank gestured with his chin toward the case he held. "If anything happened to me—and the chances of that are better than the chances of me getting rich—she'd have no one to take care of her. I surmised making a modest investment in a successful mining operation could provide enough steady income she wouldn't have to worry. Not riches, sir. I'm hoping to provide her with security."

Hardt's movement suggested he'd put his hands on his hips. "Are you willing to invest your life in something bigger than yourself in order to see that happen?"

Surprisingly, Hardt had summed up Hank's plan for his life—investing it in something bigger and having a higher purpose. But he'd feared he would never again have the chance to realize that dream. "Yes, I am. I'm willing to do anything."

"Then find a way to meet those requirements."

If only it were that easy.

"I don't happen to have a bride packed in my suitcase," Hank said dryly.

The mayor laughed. "No, I reckon she wouldn't fit in between those cards. However, I happen to know an unattached young lady who recently moved to town, Miss Ophelia Rathbone. She comes from a well-connected Denver family. She'd make some lucky man a fine wife."

Hank didn't consider himself a lucky man. At least, he hadn't been over the past seven years. "With all the single men pouring in, I'm surprised someone hasn't snatched her up."

"She hasn't found the right one yet."

Hardt's remark echoed an earlier comment from Hammond and called to mind the reverend's parting remarks, something about taking a package off his hands. Had he meant the woman? If so, what was wrong with her?

"If you'd like, I'll arrange an introduction," the mayor added in a tone a mite too casual. "In the meantime, if you're still looking for a place to stay, rent one of the rooms above the Golden Nugget."

"I inquired about one, but the barkeeper said there weren't any available."

"Tell Seamus I referred you. He'll find you a room."

"All right then," Hank replied. "Thank you, sir."

Talk about luck! Somehow, he'd managed to impress this influential man enough to get one of the few rooms in town *and* gain an introduction to an eligible lady. It couldn't hurt to meet Miss Rathbone. If she turned out to be ugly, what did that matter to someone who couldn't see? But once the young lady met *him*, would she even consider marrying a blind man? He supposed that was a bridge he'd cross when he came to it.

Would she smell like orange blossoms?

The thought came out of nowhere and Hank chided himself. He had to stop dwelling on a woman who sold her body, and start thinking about wooing an upright lady who could possibly be his future wife. "I'd be pleased to make Miss Rathbone's acquaintance."

Hardt clapped him on the back. "Good. You won't be sorry."

"No, I can't imagine I will be."

CHAPTER 4

*C*obb's Penn, the only Dry Goods store in Noelle, had become a favorite gathering place for the newly married ladies. Jolie kept her eyes fixed straight ahead as she entered the store, pretending not to notice the curious—and judgmental—glances. Back before the wagonload of brides had shown up and the majority of females in town were women like her, she had loved coming into the store and browsing. These days, she dreaded shopping here.

Among the customers in the crowded store were the two women who'd earlier been at the abandoned building across from *La Maison*. Mrs. Hammond, and the other disgustingly beautiful woman, were huddled together over at a display of homemaking products, the kind of things someone might need if they were going to cook or clean, or any number of things Jolie hated to do. She ignored their rude stares as she went over to the case that held the cosmetics she favored, and to find a tinting lotion that would turn her hair a titillating shade of auburn. They might even have a bottle of her favorite perfume.

Hank's compliment on her fragrance kept coming back to her, as did his dimpled smile and the shifting emotions reflected in his sparkling blue eyes. For a man who couldn't see, he certainly said a lot with a look and a touch. When he'd gently traced her features, her knees had nearly buckled. She'd meant to put him out of her mind...if her mind would cooperate. As soon as she got back to business, she'd forget about him.

She stared through the glass at the items in the case. *Hold on, this wasn't right. What were those baby rattles and bibs doing in there?* Jolie looked accusingly at the proprietor's wife, who was waiting on another customer.

Avis Fulton was the daughter of the former madam at *La Maison*, who had abandoned her at a young age. Although the two appeared to have made peace, there were bound to be unresolved issues. Maybe this was Avis's way of getting revenge. But she'd never been hateful to the girls who worked at the parlor house. She'd even befriended Angelique. No, Avis wasn't mean and vindictive. This change in merchandise had to do with the brides' arrival. Liam Fulton paid close attention to what his customers asked for, and of course, these women would be having babies soon.

At the twinge of pain, Jolie put her hand to her abdomen. Her mind was playing cruel tricks on her again. It had been over four years. She could no longer feel the same pain she'd felt after losing a child. Not only that, Doc Deane had informed her she was likely sterile on account of the carbolic acid she used to prevent disease. She would be having no blue-eyed babies.

She spun away from the counter. *Stupid. What nonsense.* She didn't want that blue-eyed smooth-talker, and she didn't want his babies either.

"Jolie," Avis called out as she walked past. "If you're looking for the cosmetics, we've moved them up here." Avis offered a friendly smile as Jolie approached. "What can I get for you?"

Iridescent skin, jet-black hair, lovely dark eyes, Avis had no need for cosmetics or hair treatments. In spite of her astounding beauty, a stupid, cruel man had rejected and belittled her because of her parentage, something she couldn't control and didn't matter anyway. But she'd eventually found acceptance in Noelle, and a husband whose unwavering love surrounded her with a hedge of protection. As Hank had suggested, faithful men did exist, though they were extremely rare.

Jolie perused the items in the front counter. "I'll take the rouge, the Parisian hair cream, and a package of Adam's chewing gum. Thank you." While Avis tallied up the cost, Jolie opened the beaded bag she kept tied around her waist.

Avis made eye contact, before she shifted her glance in the direction where Mrs. Hammond and her friend still lingered, then handed Jolie a sack containing her items, along with a copy of the newspaper. "Don't forget this! You'll want to read page two," she added in a low voice,

The newspaper? Jolie took it, despite not having asked for it, and went outside to head back home. Avis seemed eager for her to read something. Some gossip, perhaps? The new editor didn't generally report on anything very interesting, mostly about politics and issues having to do with the new silver mine and construction of the railroad, which they kept saying was coming soon.

She glanced at the masthead, which featured an illustration of an American flag draped over a townscape representing Noelle. The artist had left out *La Maison*. Jolie assumed it wasn't an oversight. Pearl would've drawn it in.

Should she and Draven decide to start a competing newspaper with that printer they owned, it would have a much prettier masthead—and more interesting news.

As soon as she opened the door to the house, she heard one of the girls upstairs hollering for Angelique to bring her breakfast. Jolie veered into the parlor and checked the clock on the mantle. Four already, and Felice wasn't even out of bed. She always had an excuse for why she couldn't get up in time to help around the house.

Angelique burst through the door leading from the kitchen.

"Don't you go up there!" Jolie blocked her way to the staircase. "Why are you letting her boss you around?"

Angelique looked away. Wasn't hard to figure out that Felice had either bribed or blackmailed her, if indeed Felice really knew anything. Angelique didn't talk and she didn't keep journals, she might not even know how to read or write. Whatever the reason, Jolie knew how it felt to be vulnerable, and to fear someone would let out your secrets.

"You come to me if you have any problems with her." Without thinking, she gave Angelique a hug.

When the girl gasped, Jolie stepped back, being just as surprised by her actions. She didn't get sentimental, and she didn't like to touch or be touched, so what had set off that display of affection?

Angelique's dark brows gathered in a look of worried confusion.

"No, I'm not losing my mind. Just go back to what you were doing. Helping Milly cook?"

Angelique nodded.

"She had better watch out, or you'll get her job."

Jolie was rewarded with a quick smile that made her heart constrict, but she refrained from giving Angelique another hug. She wasn't the girl's mother; she wasn't even that much older. "We have enough claret for tonight? You've checked on the whiskey? What about Solomon's favorite tobacco?"

Angelique gave her a thumbs-up before heading back to the kitchen.

Jolie walked over to the staircase and yelled: "Felice, get your lazy bones out of bed! No one's bringing you coffee. Not Milly not Angelique, and certainly not me."

With a harrumph, she sat in the cushioned chair next to the fireplace and opened the newspaper.

Crusading Ladies Start Petition to Rid Noelle of Vice

The headline leapt out at her. The story beneath it took her breath away. The pastor's wife, Mrs. Hammond, and another woman, Miss Ophelia Rathbone, had started circulating a petition in town that called for shutting down the brothels, starting with *La Maison*.

Meddling do-gooders! That explained why those women had been sneaking around across the street, spying and plotting trouble, making a fuss, trying to tell everyone how to live their lives. The men of Noelle wouldn't let two so-called *crusading ladies* shut down their favorite place for entertainment and relaxation.

The image of baby rattles and bibs popped into Jolie's head.

Jolie leapt to her feet, flung the newspaper aside, and began to pace in front of the fireplace. What was happening in Noelle? Had the brides cast a spell over all the men in town? No, not *all* the men. They'd turned the heads of the most influential and respected men, the ones who would steer the town into the future—a future that didn't include women like Jolie.

"This *can't* happen!"

"What can't happen?" Felice slumped onto the couch, her eyes still at half-mast. She'd slipped into a silk robe with nothing underneath. The aspiring actress-turned-prostitute liked showing off her body to anyone who happened to be around. There was no one at the moment to appreciate it.

A wry smile pulled at Jolie's lips. Felice and the preacher's wife, Felicity, had similar names, although they couldn't be more different. "The preacher's wife and some other self-righteous prude, Miss Rathbone, are trying to shut us down. They've been using that abandoned building to spy on us. Now they're circulating a petition to make our business illegal." Jolie picked up the paper and thrust it at Felice. "Here's an article in the newspaper about it."

Felice waved away the paper. "I don't know how to read."

Many women didn't. Being able to read was an advantage Jolie had over the others who might want to take her position. But what good would it do her if the town shut down the house, and those crusaders drove the prostitutes out? They'd have to start over somewhere else, and Jolie didn't have enough saved. She'd reached the pinnacle of her profession as the madam of a fancy parlor house. Would she now be relegated to starting over as a working girl in some other madam's parlor house, or worse, in a saloon?

"We have to *do* something."

"Ask the men who are coming here tonight to help us," Felice suggested. "Aren't they rich and influential?"

"And married, plus involved in politics. Richard Stiles and Solomon Sharp won't risk their railroad jobs and their reputations for the likes of us. I'll have to go to someone who doesn't care what people think." Jolie whirled about and held up her finger, inspired by the only idea she could come up with. "I know, I'll ask Sheriff Draven. Pearl used to work here. He understands how it is. He'll help us."

CHAPTER 5

*T*he next morning, Hank left his room at the Golden Nugget, which had been miraculously provided due to Mr. Hardt's influence. After locating the barber, he got a haircut and shave, and had requested an extra splash of cologne. He'd need all the help he could get, if he hoped to win over Ophelia Rathbone. That is, once he met her.

Mr. Hardt had come by for a drink the previous evening and had issued an invitation for dinner the next day at his home up on the mountain. Charlie, as he'd insisted on being called, had even offered to come by in the wagon and give Hank a ride. The mayor was being so accommodating, Hank worried Miss Rathbone had a more serious defect than he'd originally imagined.

"Can't afford to be picky," he said to Bear as they exited the barber's shop. He stopped outside to get his bearings. Charlie had graciously described the layout of the town, explaining it in a way that made it easy for Hank to picture, and fortunately, he had excellent memory.

Across the street, the sheriff's office and jail, to the right

37

of that, the dry goods and grocery store. Jolie had suggested the proprietor might be interested in Hank's cards.

Hank smelled tortillas cooking, which was an improvement over the ever-present odor of muck and manure. The delicious smell would be coming from Nacho's diner, just beyond the barbershop. Further on to the left, the road split off and snaked through a small valley, which Hardt had called the entertainment district. Down that road were the brothels, the first and fanciest being *La Maison*.

Hank lingered a moment, wondering what Jolie might be doing after spending an evening entertaining guests. He tamped down a flare of jealousy, which was absolutely absurd. She was a madam, a prostitute. Besides, she'd walked away from him, which as it turned out was for the better. She knew it as well as he did.

"Hank!" Jolie called to him, as if he'd conjured her just by thinking of her.

He jerked and saw a shape a moment before she flung her arms around his neck and gave him a kiss on the cheek. He was so stunned he just stood stock still, his senses awash in the sweet scent of orange blossoms.

"Oh, it's so good to see you! I needed to meet a friendly face this morning."

Hank retained his hold on Bear's leash and on the handle of the case containing his cards. With both hands occupied, he had an excuse for not returning the hug, even though hugging her seemed a response as natural as breathing. But there was no telling who might be nearby, and what they'd report and to whom, so it wouldn't be wise to add fuel to gossip that might circulate, ruining his chances to win a respectable bride and meet Mr. Hardt's requirements.

"Hank? What's wrong?" Jolie's arms slid away, leaving him feeling guilty and strangely bereft.

"Nothing, you just surprised me. I didn't expect you to be out this early."

"I wouldn't be if I wasn't in danger of losing my home!" Underlying her angry retort, he heard real fear.

"Losing your home?" He set down his case and put his arm out, and she didn't hesitate to come into his embrace. She put her head on his shoulder and her hands to his chest, seeking protection. At the moment, there was nothing he wanted more than to shelter her from harm. "Tell me what happened."

"Some meddling women are circulating a petition that calls for shutting down the brothels, starting with *La Maison*. From what I heard our customers say last night, they may succeed if they rally the other married ladies."

"I'm sorry to hear it." Hank didn't know what else to say. So that's what the barber must've been talking about when he'd grumbled about interfering women. Hank had been more interested in gossip about the silver mine.

The creak of wagon wheels came closer. Snatches of conversations drifted over when a door creaked opened and men exited the nearby diner, their voices fading to low murmurs as they walked in the other direction.

Hank swallowed his nervousness. He longed to help Jolie, but what could *he* do? He had no influence in this town, and if he aligned himself behind her cause, he might as well kiss his chances of winning Miss Rathbone goodbye, along with his dream of investing in the town's largest silver mine.

She patted his chest. "You look very nice, and you smell nice. Were you on your way over to *La Maison*?"

The thought had crossed his mind.

"No, I was on my way to see if I could sell these cards to Mr. Fulton."

"Is that Liam's favorite cologne?" Jolie teased.

Guilt lashed Hank from all directions. He forced himself to let her go. "I wish I could help you."

Her head moved on his shoulder as she looked up at him. Although he couldn't see her face, he suspected she was frowning with confusion at his mixed signals. She stepped back and cold air filled the vacant space between them. "No, I don't expect that you could do anything. I'm on my way to see the sheriff. He has some influence with Mr. Hardt."

Her response slashed at Hank's conscience more than his pride. He wasn't surprised she'd flung that remark about his lack of importance in the community after he'd made it clear he wouldn't help her. But she had no idea what had transpired since yesterday, and he had no desire to elaborate. On the other hand, he felt he owed her an explanation, simply because he'd led her to believe they could be friends.

"Well, I'll leave you to your business." She set off across the street before he could work up the courage to explain.

Hank gave Bear a signal to follow her, and they trudged behind her through the mud. They had to cross the street anyway, because the general store was next to the sheriff's office. With the aid of bright daylight, he could make out the shapes of buildings, and he could see Jolie's small form a few feet ahead.

Bear hesitated after they crossed the road, but Hank urged him on, not paying close attention, and tripped as his foot found the edge of the boardwalk. He managed to catch himself, fortunately.

Jolie hadn't stopped. Either she hadn't seen him stumble, or she didn't want him following her.

"Sheriff Draven!" she called out. "Can I talk to you?"

The person moving toward her appeared to be a big man. "You're out early."

"Is everyone aware of my schedule?" Her curt reply sounded as if she'd directed it over her shoulder.

Bear had continued to follow her, but then the dog suddenly stopped and growled.

Hank froze. Bear only did that when danger threatened.

The sound of another growl came from just beyond Jolie. Another dog? No, that was the *man* growling, the sheriff!

Bear backed away and slunk behind Hank, to his utter astonishment.

"Draven, stop baring your teeth and scaring poor Bear," Jolie scolded the sheriff. "This is Hank Donovan. He's a traveling salesman and he's on his way to see Liam. Hank, this is Draven, our sheriff. He has a scar that cuts across his face and he's missing one eye, and he looks terrifying. But he's really a big softie."

"I'm not a softie. And that dog growled first," the sheriff rumbled.

"Nice to meet you, Sheriff." Hank stepped forward and put his hand out. He figured he ought to get into the lawman's good graces before he and Bear were both run out of town.

The sheriff grunted a greeting and shook Hank's hand. Bear came out from behind Hank's leg with a low growl still rumbling in his throat.

"Mind your manners." Hank had to get firm with the dog. Bear was behaving like a child. Hopefully, the sheriff would start acting his age as well. "Shake. Shake the sheriff's hand."

"Well, I'll be." Draven's inflection conveyed awe. He probably hadn't expected the growling dog to sit down and placidly hold up his paw. Hank had worked hard to train Bear so that he'd be accepted and not feared, with the exception of those who sought to do Hank harm, and this sheriff didn't appear to be among that ilk.

"Take his paw, Draven. He won't bite," Jolie said in a laughing tone. "Pearl, come meet Bear!"

Jolie introduced Bear to the other woman, who turned out to be the sheriff's wife, and then introduced Hank. He clearly came second in her affections behind his dog.

"What brings you out so early?" Pearl's question was no doubt directed at Jolie. Hank smiled, imagining her reaction, and knowing the repeated greeting was rubbing thin.

"Did you see the newspaper article yesterday?" Jolie asked. "The one about the petition to shut down the brothels, starting with *La Maison*?"

"I did." Pearl's voice became solemn. "I showed it to Draven."

"That's what happens when towns get civilized." Draven's tone implied he didn't much care for the *civilizing* influences.

"Sheriff, Mr. Hardt respects you. Will you talk to him and convince him to stop this?" Jolie continued.

"Sure, I can talk to him, but he won't stop it if his wife supports it."

"The article didn't name Mrs. Hardt. It said Mrs. Hammond and some new woman in town, I think her name is Ophelia Rathbone, are behind the petition."

Hank's breath caught. The woman Charlie wanted him

42

to court was crusading to close down Jolie's home and business? When Jolie found out he intended to court Ophelia, she would hate him with a passion.

That may be, but he owed his sister a better life, and this was the only chance he'd get to do something about it. Now, he just had to be brave enough and considerate enough to tell Jolie. She deserved to hear it from him first. After tonight, word would spread fast.

"Excuse me, Sheriff and Mrs." He hadn't been given their last name. "It was very nice to meet you. Jolie, may I have a word with you?"

After a brief silence—he imagined she was surprised at the request—she bid her friends farewell, then took his arm and walked with him toward the store.

With every step, Hank's dread increased. "Can you find us a spot to have a private conversation?"

"Go left into the alley between the buildings," she suggested.

He sent Bear into the dark space and after they'd gone a few steps, Jolie stopped him.

"What is it, Hank? What's wrong?"

He set his case on the ground, took a deep breath, and began, "I met with Mr. Hardt yesterday."

"How did it go?"

"Ah, well, as you said, he seems to be a fair-minded man. He told me he would consider allowing me to invest if I could meet three requirements." Hank counted them off on his fingers. "One, settle here in Noelle. Two, maintain an upright reputation, and three—get married."

"Which means you need to stay away from me." Her fingers squeezed his upper arm, then slid away. The hurt in her voice made the separation worse, and the fact she so willingly accepted his rejection made it even more so.

"I'm sorry." He'd managed two more words, now for the rest.

"You don't have to apologize, Hank. I knew you'd need to fit in with the Hardts and people like them, that's why I walked away yesterday. I'm not the type of woman you escort around town."

He didn't want her to think he considered her below other women. "I'd be proud to escort you, and it wouldn't bother me a bit if I didn't—"

"If you didn't have to meet those requirements. No need to explain. You must get in on that silver mine so you won't have to worry about how you'll support your sister. Maybe she and her family can move out here. That would be nice, wouldn't it, being able to bring your family together?"

The longing in Jolie's voice tore at Hank's heart. Where was her family? Had she been abandoned, abused, lured out West with promises...he'd heard all kinds of horror stories. This wasn't the time to ask those questions, and knowing the answers wouldn't make it easier for him to say what he had to say. "There's something else I need to tell you. Mr. Hardt offered to introduce me to an available young lady who's seeking a husband."

"She's lucky."

"No. *I'm* lucky, if she—or any woman—will have me, considering my condition."

"And *I* stand by what I said. She's lucky."

Jolie's affirmation only twisted the knife she'd unknowingly slipped between his ribs when she'd encouraged him to marry and reunite his family. How could she be so kind and understanding, especially when he'd just confirmed what she thought, that she wasn't worthy of him. Those were society's perceptions, not his. But what good would it do to explain when it changed nothing, and only made him sound like a hypocrite?

Hank took a deep breath. "The woman I'll be meeting tonight...is Miss Ophelia Rathbone."

"What!" Jolie screeched. She recoiled as if he'd just announced he'd contracted a disease.

He could plead for her understanding and forgiveness, yet she had no reason to offer it to him. "Apparently, Mr. Hardt is eager to see this young lady wed, and now it makes sense. I suspect it's on account of her involvement in this cause, and she and Mrs. Hammond stirring things up. Maybe I can convince her to—"

"Stay home and make babies? That's a great idea, Hank. Good luck."

"That's not what I—"

Jolie whirled around and left the dark alley, bright daylight outlining her retreating form. Before she rounded the corner, she called out, "Liam Fulton's store is on your left. When you enter, there's a high threshold, so watch your step."

She was still concerned for his safety. Even after he'd told he would betray her in the worst possible way, by pursing her enemy.

Guilt-stricken, Hank dropped to one knee and put his arm across Bear's shoulders. The dog nosed him and whined. "I know, I want to go after her too, but we can't."

He had to remember why he was doing this. His sister, his nephew and niece, they depended on him. He was doing the right thing.

So why did he feel he'd just made the worst mistake of his life?

Jolie ran without looking back. Even if she had looked back, Hank couldn't see her well enough to see her tears. He couldn't see the expression of shock and heartbreak she couldn't keep off her face.

She drew her scarf higher to block the cold wind. As much as she hated the thought of Hank marrying that Ophelia woman, she couldn't despise him for it. He'd do what he had to do to secure his family's future, just as she'd done what she had to do to survive.

Not only that, but Hank was the marrying type. He was the kind of man who'd be faithful to his wife and kind to his children. He wasn't the type of man who could love a woman like her. She'd known he wouldn't be around for long, so she had only herself to blame for being foolish about him.

"Jolie! Wait!"

She heard the sound of crunching ice and turned to see Pearl, also bundled against the cold, coming from the sheriff's office. "You left before I could tell you I'll try to help."

Jolie dashed away her tears. "Thank you."

Pearl's china blue eyes widened with a look of astonishment, which didn't surprise Jolie. Unlike most women, she didn't break into tears over every little disappointment, because it was pointless. All those tears she'd shed four years ago had done her no good.

Pearl's startled expression melted into genuine concern. "What's wrong?"

Sweet, gentle Pearl. It was a good thing Draven had wed her. She wasn't hardened enough to survive long-term in the business. Women engaged in prostitution didn't have long life spans, and those like Pearl were chewed up and spit out faster than most.

"What do you think is wrong? I'm worried we'll be thrown out."

"That's why you're crying?"

Turning to continue to the corner, Jolie tugged her hood down and brought the scarf up just below her eyes so her face wouldn't be an open book. When had she gotten so bad at hiding her emotions? When she'd met Hank, that's when. Somehow, he'd found an opening in her defenses and pried open her heart enough to gain her sympathy.

Pearl slipped her arm through Jolie's, slowing her down. "I can't believe Mrs. Hardt would let them throw you out. She doesn't have a mean bone in her body."

"Misguided goodness can be just as cruel."

"I suspect this uproar will blow over."

"Not with those two crusaders running around stirring things up." And Hank wanted to marry one of them! Actually, he hadn't acted all that thrilled with the prospect. He'd been offered what he thought was his only chance to win a respectable bride.

Would Ophelia find him pitiable? Jolie harrumphed. Any woman should consider herself fortunate to have Hank as her husband.

"I'll also speak with Genevieve Kinnison," Pearl continued. "Perhaps she can rope in those two energetic young women and involve them with planning the new mission that she and Penny are starting here in Noelle. They want to help more women like us find husbands."

"Women like us?" Jolie scoffed. "You mean prostitutes?"

"Women in trouble, those whom society has rejected, or who've been reduced to poverty. Like all those brides Genevieve brought here from the mission in Denver. Don't you remember?

"How could I forget? They evicted us."

"Those women didn't evict us. The pastor and Mr. Hardt thought it best if we moved our business across the street while the single women were staying at *La Maison*. Which you have to agree was really the only way it would work."

Jolie halted at the end of the boardwalk. She hated to admit Pearl was right, but she had too much common sense to argue, although, at the time, she'd been resentful. In some cases, downright mean. She winced as she recalled how nasty she'd been to the doctor's new wife.

"Do you think Felicity Hammond is doing this because of how I treated those women when they moved in?"

"She doesn't strike me as vindictive," Pearl mused.

"I wasn't nice." Jolie admitted for the first time what she'd been unable to find the courage to say before now. "And I wasn't very nice to you either, or anyone else. You're kind and generous, and you know how to make people feel cared for and special. I'm just the opposite. That's why I had to learn more tricks."

And that was why she would never have a good man like Hank.

Pearl's gaze softened. "Jolie, dear, you have a very tender heart. You just need to let people see that."

Jolie's eyes started to sting. "Why? So they can crush it?"

She pulled her arm from Pearl's grasp and ran across the street, nearly colliding with a wagon and drawing a loud curse from the driver. Perhaps being kind worked for Pearl, but Jolie knew better than to think changing her ways would make any difference in how she was perceived. The best she could hope for would be to stay in Noelle and run *La Maison*, and the sooner she stopped feeling sorry for herself, the better.

As she hurried past the abandoned house, she caught a glimpse of someone entering the front door. Her despair flared into anger. Those two nosy women must've come back. She decided she would go over there and give them a piece of her mind.

Jolie slipped inside the old log building that faced *La Maison*. The inside looked as if little had changed from when she and other girls had been temporary occupants over Christmas; it had the same worn furnishings and chinked walls. She'd heard rumors another brothel would soon open here, but the kind of women she'd seen hanging around weren't whores.

Mounting the stairs, she followed the sound of voices to an upper room, which had served as an entertaining parlor. She didn't knock, just walked through the open door.

The faded curtains were drawn back, letting light shine through clean glass panes. Two prim ladies in drab gray gowns perched on the faded red velvet settee. Two younger women, more fashionably attired, occupied cushioned chairs that had seen much use.

The last time Jolie had been in here, a roomful of miners had been chasing her and the other girls around, and one of the chair legs had broken. Someone apparently fixed it since then.

The prudish women on the settee she recognized as Mrs. Sharp and Mrs. Stiles, the wives of two of the influential railroad men who'd been at *La Maison* the previous night. The younger women were the preacher's new bride, Felicity Hammond and...*Ophelia Rathbone*. Had to be. She was the prettiest woman in the room.

The four women stared at Jolie with expressions ranging from horror to surprise to outright curiosity.

"What are you doing here?" Jolie demanded. "This is private property." The building didn't belong to her, but it didn't belong to them either.

Mrs. Hammond was the first to recover her wits. "Yes, we know that. This building belongs to Mr. Hardt. He's allowed us its use for our meetings."

"What meetings?"

"A commission to abolish *immoral* activities that pose a danger to our community," Mrs. Sharp shot back.

The preacher's wife leapt to her feet. "Yes, but we aren't *only* concerned with improving men's morals. We must see to the well-being of the women in our community."

"That's right! We're concerned about the plight of the women in Noelle." Ophelia piped in with a look of wide-eyed innocence.

She really did have lovely eyes, a unique shade of violet-blue. Jolie longed to scratch them out. "You don't look like you're suffering from a plight."

Miss Rathbone had the audacity to look wounded. "I am suffering just like these other women, and you. We lack personal freedoms and rights that should be ours. We women have no voice because we have no vote. We're made in God's image too, and we should be given an equal say in how this town and state, and even this country are run."

Jolie propped her hands on her hips and aimed her scowl at Ophelia. "What does that have to do with kicking me out of my house?

Ophelia glanced around the room, but no one else seemed interested in explaining. "Brothels are places of bondage where men use women for pleasure. It's a form of slavery. I should think you would agree?"

"No, I don't agree," Jolie fired back. "We have plenty of freedom." *Except for the freedom to fall in love and marry men like Hank.* But she'd lost that opportunity due to her own decisions, so she wouldn't whine about it.

Mrs. Stiles came to her feet and pointed a plump finger

at Jolie. "You and those hussies have tempted our husbands and made them fall into sin."

Jolie snorted. "We don't *make* them do anything. They come to us because they want to buy what we have to sell. I suppose they aren't getting it at home."

Mrs. Stiles put her hand to her chest as if she was about to swoon, and the woman seated next to her, Mrs. Sharp, helped her sit down. "There, there, Gertie. We'll be rid of them soon enough."

Jolie swept a hard gaze over the so-called committee. "If your men are straying, getting rid of us isn't going to make them stop, and turning us into criminals won't make you better. You have no idea what it's like to be abandoned, or to go hungry, or to wonder whether you'll have a roof over your head, much less a warm, comfortable bed. Whatever we have, we've worked hard for it, and I'm not letting meddling biddies like you take everything away without a fight!"

CHAPTER 6

*a*fter selling his inventory, Hank took his money as the shopkeeper counted it out, then folded the greenbacks and pocketed them. "Thank you, Mr. Fulton."

"Call me Liam. And it's a pleasure doing business with you, Hank Donovan. If these Valentine cards sell as well as I think they will, we'll want twice as many for next year."

"Twice as many?" Hank closed up the empty case on the counter, thanking his lucky stars for aligning. "Of course! I'll put in your order and personally deliver the next shipment."

"Maybe you should think of moving your card business here to Noelle," Liam advised. "This is a good place to raise a family."

"So I've heard." Hank's euphoria wavered at the memory of the last thing Jolie had said to him about distracting his future wife by making babies. He wasn't as excited at the idea as he thought he might be. Once he'd met Ophelia, he might feel differently. "Have a good day, Liam."

"Good luck with your courting, Hank."

"How did you know I was...?"

"All that cologne you're wearing, for one, and word

spreads fast around town. I heard you'll be joining the Hardts and the Hammonds for dinner tonight, and a certain Miss will be in attendance."

"So they say. I appreciate the well wishes." Hank closed his empty suitcase and tried to drum up enthusiasm at the idea of meeting Ophelia Rathbone. Instead, his mind kept wandering back to the alley and the hurt in Jolie's voice.

"Here let me get the door," Liam offered. "Nice dog you got there."

"Thanks for letting me bring him inside. I'd hate to think what might've happened to your displays otherwise."

Liam's chuckle followed Hank as he left.

He stood at the edge of the sidewalk and recalled the map he'd drawn in his head. Just across the street and a few doors down was the diner. He'd go over there and have some of those tortillas he smelled cooking and share his meal with Bear. The dog had to be hungry. Afterwards, they'd go back to the room and retrieve the card he'd saved for Ophelia, then meet Mr. Hardt outside the Golden Nugget as arranged.

He should be elated. Everything was going not just according to plan, but better than he'd hoped. With the extra income he'd make from a share in the silver mine, he could move his family out here and their card business. His sister could still do the designs, and they could afford to hire other women to help her produce them.

Bear led him safely across the street, and after they'd gone a short distance down the boardwalk, he could make out more people milling about.

"Maybe they're going to get something to eat too." He patted his dog.

"Ja-zus, would ya look at that thing!" a man exclaimed. "Ugliest beast I ever seen."

Hank frowned, recognizing the voice as one of the miners who'd been teasing Bear the day before when Hank had gone into the Golden Nugget to inquire about renting a room. The miner and his friends had taunted the dog into reacting, and when Bear growled, they'd complained. The barkeeper had politely asked Hank to take the dog elsewhere.

Best to avoid the troublemaker.

When Hank pulled Bear toward the building, someone in front of them moved quickly and let out a high, fearful cry, alerting Hank to the fact it was a woman.

"He won't hurt you, ma'am," Hank assured her. "Is this the diner?"

"Y-yes, it is. They don't allow dogs inside."

Hank hoped he could convince the owner to make an exception. He didn't want to end up falling over a table or knocking someone's meal into their lap. Hank moved closer and groped for a handle or knob.

From the inside, someone shoved the door outward, sending Hank stumbling backwards, falling back into the woman he'd just met. Bear wedged his body in between them, and the woman's scream pierced Hank's ears.

"Hey, get that thing away from her!"

"Help the lady!"

"Watch out, it might bite!"

Men's voices came from all directions, confusing Hank as to which way he should be facing. "It's all right," he called out. "Bear won't hurt anybody."

"Ned, git aholt of that beast. Don't let it bite ya."

Someone lunged toward Hank and yanked at the dog's leash.

"Let *go*," Hank demanded, holding tight. "I can control him."

"The hell you can." The man who'd been jerking on the leash shoved at Hank's chest, and Bear gave a warning growl.

"Git back! It's attackin'!"

A shot rang out.

Bear's yelp of pain sent an ice-cold shock straight through Hank. The leash grew taut, as if the dog had lost his footing.

"No!" Hank dropped to his knees, stretching his arms out, shielding the whimpering dog with his own body. "Stop shooting you idiots! He's not dangerous!"

Disbelieving murmurs came from the crowd that now hovered around him. The stench of gunpowder mingled with the smell of manure and the faint scent of blood, all of which sent Hank's stomach roiling.

"For God's sake..." His voice trembled with rage and fear. "Don't kill my dog."

"Looked to me like it was attackin.' Ned just took hold of the leash and that dog started growlin'."

The miner. Had he been the one to shoot Bear? Hank longed to throw himself at the wretched scoundrel and beat him to a pulp, but he wasn't willing to move away from his dog in case someone decided to start shooting again.

"He was trying to protect me, you damn fool!" Hank cradled the big dog protectively. "Could somebody help us?"

He looked around at the retreating figures, hearing ice-encrusted mud crunch as people walked away. They were cowards, or they didn't care. To hell with them!

Hank stroked Bear's face and the dog whimpered and licked his hand. *God, oh God...* Bear could be bleeding to death. Running his fingers over the dog's thick coat, he anxiously searched for the bullet wound. "Where is it? Where did you get hit?"

"Mister, are you hurt?" A heavy hand clasped Hank shoulder, and the man's deep voice conveyed concern. Thank God someone had bothered to stop.

"It's my dog," Hank choked out. "Some trigger-happy fool shot him, but I can't see well enough to tell how badly he's injured."

"He's favoring his back leg and there's blood on his hindquarters. I'll bet Woody can fix him up. You got a wagon?"

"No."

"We can load him into mine and take him up to the barn."

Hank didn't know a thing about the barn, or Woody, and he wasn't sure he trusted another stranger after what just happened. If he could just see better, he'd know what to do to help Bear. Jolie could see, and they weren't that far from the house.

"Take us to *La Maison*." Hank slipped his arms beneath Bear and lifted, being as careful as possible. The dog's legs dangled and he whimpered. "I've got you, boy. It'll be all right."

"He looks heavy. I could carry him," the Good Samaritan offered.

Hank secured his hold on the big dog. Did it look like he couldn't manage on his own? "No, I'll do it. If you guide me to your wagon, I'll put him in there and ride with him."

After loading Bear into the wagon bed, Hank climbed in. He held the dog partly on his lap to cushion the rough ride. It struck Hank he hadn't introduced himself. "I'm Hank Donovan. Thank you for your help."

"Culver Daniels, happy to be of assistance. I'm sorry I arrived too late to stop them from shooting your dog."

"Bear wouldn't have hurt anyone. He only growled to

warn them off." He ran his hand over the dog's silky ears, and an overwhelming grief squeezed his heart, followed by the gut-wrenching awareness of his situation.

Without Culver's assistance he couldn't have gotten Bear to safety. What had given him the crazy idea to come out here on his own, or to think that he could be useful to anyone? He couldn't even protect his own dog.

It took far longer to reach the parlor house by wagon than it had taken Hank to return to town on foot, or maybe fear was making time drag. Whining, Bear twisted in his arms, trying to reach the injury, no doubt to lick at it, as dogs were wont to do.

"Lie still, boy. We'll soon be somewhere we can get you fixed up." Hank spoke in low, soothing tones and continued to pet the dog. If a bullet had lodged in Bear's hindquarters, it would have to be removed, and the wound cleansed and stitched.

"We're at *La Maison*," Culver announced, bringing the wagon to a stop.

Hank climbed out and lifted Bear into his arms. Culver helped guide him to the front door, then knocked. A click sounded, and as the door opened, Hank smelled the faint scent of orange blossoms. Just knowing Jolie was there calmed him.

"Hank?" she gasped. "My God! What happened?"

"Bear's been shot. We need your help." He didn't doubt for a moment she'd help him, even though he'd given her no reason to be gracious.

"Of course, come in!" Jolie moved away from the entrance to let Hank inside. "Can you see me well enough to follow?"

He squinted at the fuzzy outline of her shape. "Yes."

"We'll take him to the back parlor. It's warmer there."

Hank followed her down the hallway to a room with better lighting. He could see the shapes of other people moving around, and it wasn't long before he heard a gasp.

"What are you bringing in here?" a woman's voice—screechy, like an out-of-tune violin—asked. It appeared another person was with her, but she—or he—didn't say anything.

"Calm down, Felice. Someone shot Hank's dog and Bear needs tending."

Hank brushed against a piece of furniture, but Jolie stayed close enough to prevent him from banging into anything. He felt warmth in the air and then she touched his arm.

"This is a good place," she said. "Close enough to the wood stove to keep him warm."

Hank settled the dog onto the carpeted floor and Jolie knelt beside him. "He may be bleeding. I'll pay to replace the rug."

"Nonsense. We can clean it if we have to."

A swish of skirts came from behind them, accompanied by the smell of cloying perfume. "You should've taken it to a barn. That creature doesn't belong in here."

Hank put the voice with a name Jolie had used previously—*Felice*. Didn't that mean *happy*? Not in this case apparently.

"Be helpful for once," Jolie responded. "Go get an old blanket, and some water and rags."

Hank ticked off what else they'd need. "Also small scissors, tweezers, a needle and silk thread, and some of that carbolic acid solution, tincture of opium, if you have it—"

"I'm not a servant," the other woman snipped. "Ask Angelique."

"She's not a servant either, in case that fact happened to

slip your mind," Jolie shot back. "Will you please just get what Hank asked for?"

"*You* get it. Come on, Angelique. We'll soon have customers to see to. Let Jolie take care of the dog."

The uppity whore left the room, and he assumed the silent woman went with her.

Jolie sighed. "Never mind her. I'll take care of it."

Hank hadn't considered how his appearance might disrupt their business, and it humbled him to realize Jolie cared enough to set aside other priorities. "I'm sorry to trouble you. Thank you for helping us."

"You aren't troubling me, Hank." She sounded weary, but sincere. As she stood, her skirt brushed his shoulder. "I'll go get the water and rags, and the other things you asked for."

Hank didn't count the minutes, but she wasn't gone long.

"I think I have it all." Glass bottles rattled as she set something on the floor, a tray perhaps. "Angelique helped me gather everything. I can tell she's worried about Bear."

He had wondered about the silent girl. "Can Angelique speak?"

"I've never heard her utter a word. But she can hear just fine." Jolie scooted closer. "If you'll lift Bear's front, I'll position the blanket, then we can move him onto it. I brought a pitcher of water and some bowls."

"Good thinking." Hank lifted Bear and waited as Jolie spread out the blanket. "Pour some water into a bowl, add a few drops of the tincture of opium, see if he'll drink it. We need for him to relax."

Jolie set to the task he'd given her. He heard her uncork a bottle, pour water, and after a moment, she slipped the bowl beneath Bear's nose and the dog lapped at it. Hank held the bowl and petted him. In a little while, Bear stretched out.

"Looks like he's relaxed," Jolie observed. "I'll clean up that leg if he'll let me."

"I need for you to do more than that." Hank moved to cradle the dog's head in case he became agitated. "After you clean off the blood and dirt, carefully cut away the fur so you can see the wound clearly."

He heard more water being poured. "Are you sure you don't want me to send Angelique to find Woody? He's very knowledgeable about animals."

"That would take more time, who knows how much, and I can tell Bear trusts you. He might not cooperate for someone else. We need to remove the bullet and stop the bleeding—"

"Hank, I have no idea how to remove a bullet."

"I can direct you. My father was a surgeon. I helped him tend soldiers during the war and worked beside him afterwards. We removed lots of bullets." Hank projected confidence for her sake. He hadn't touched a patient since the accident, but he could recall enough to guide her. Besides, she was smart, observant, and most of all, caring.

He stroked Bear's heaving side. "He's fallen asleep, but we'll need to work fast."

"All right." She heaved a worried sigh. "I have everything spread out. Tell me what to do."

"Wipe off the scissors and tweezers with carbolic acid solution. Trim enough fur so you can see about a quarter inch of skin around the wound. Make sure there's no debris in the wound. Use the tweezers to pick it out. If it starts bleeding profusely, apply pressure with a rag."

Hank's steeled his nerves when the clipping commenced. He continued to stroke Bear's head, ready to hold Bear's muzzle if necessary, but the dog remained asleep.

"Oh! I see the bullet! It's fairly close to the surface."

What a relief they wouldn't have to dig for it. "That's good. Use the tweezers to remove it. Take your time."

When Bear whimpered, Hank cradled the dog's head.

"I got it!" Jolie cried. A clink sounded when she dropped the bullet into a container.

"Use the carbolic acid solution to clean the wound. Is it bleeding badly?"

"A little."

"Take a fresh rag and apply pressure for a moment. If the bleeding slows, that's a good sign. We won't have to cauterize. Make sure the wound is clean before you stitch it up."

"Stitch it!" She sounded horrified. "Repairing a torn sleeve isn't the same as—"

"Actually, it's not that different." It would be best if she thought so anyway. "Pinch the skin together, sew a crisscross and tie it off, then sew another one. Use your best judgment to decide how many stitches you'll need to keep the wound closed. When you're done, use a clean cloth to make a bandage and wrap the wound."

Hank stroked Bear's neck and waited. He hoped he hadn't confused her, and the silence meant she was concentrating. The seconds ticked by on a nearby clock.

"Done!" Jolie's heavy exhale made him wonder if she'd been holding her breath. He had, and now he released it.

He gently stroked Bear's head. "Thank you, Jolie. You did a good job."

"We did it together."

"Yes we did. We make a good team." Hank longed to reach out and pull her into his arms, but he didn't have that right. They weren't partners, or even close friends. In fact, they could have no ongoing relationship if he intended to court Ophelia. And he wouldn't betray either woman by marrying one, while continuing an illicit affair with the other. The only way he and Jolie could ever be together would be if he were willing to take a risk and tell Mr. Hardt he'd chosen another woman. If he did that, he'd lose his chance to invest in the silver mine for sure.

CHAPTER 7

*J*olie cleaned the scissors and set them on the tray, along with the thread, needle and bottles. Bear slept on, seemingly oblivious to Hank's continual petting. She felt a deep sense of satisfaction she'd been able to help save his dog, but she didn't fool herself into thinking she and Hank would become a *team*. He'd already gone quiet and reflective, almost as if he regretted the remark. He'd only said it out of gratitude. Earlier, he'd been clear about his plans.

Hank was a good, kind and gifted man, who deserved a chance to regain his pride in accomplishments. If it were in her power to help him, she'd do it. Her good deeds, if they could be called that, wouldn't erase her many sins, nor was she doing favors for that reason. Hank, curse him, had somehow picked the lock on her heart. She had no such claim on his.

"Aren't you supposed to meet Ophelia this evening?"

Hank ran his hand over the sleeping dog's side with concern and love written all over his face. "I won't leave Bear until I'm sure he's out of danger."

Jolie adored him all the more for his devotion to the dog. "No, of course not. Stay here as long as you like. No one comes to the back parlor except the girls, and they won't bother you tonight. I'll ask someone to get word to Mr. Hardt with your apologies."

"Thank you." Hank's smile turned wry. "It seems my debt to you is adding up."

"I'm not keeping track."

He seemed to be studying her, although she knew he couldn't see her well enough to discern the details of her form, much less her features. For that reason, she didn't even try to hide the emotions brimming in her eyes.

"Why are you here? What made you choose this life?" he asked in a solemn tone.

Jolie's heart constricted. She'd been asked the question before, and her pat answer had always been a coquettish smile and some inane remark about enjoying sex. She hadn't enjoyed sexual encounters since Asa had left her stranded and pregnant. Besides, Hank wouldn't be able to see her false smile, and she had no desire to lie to him.

"It's where I ended up because of my own decisions." Jolie heaved a sigh. This was the first time she'd admitted aloud her culpability in the matter, it being so much easier to blame others—her overbearing parents, faithless Asa and his slovenly lover. Only she'd never been able to transfer the guilt along with the blame.

Hank cocked his head, indicating another question. "What decisions?"

Oh no, she wouldn't lay bare her soul. Not to any man. "I haven't pried into your past."

"You can ask me whatever you'd like."

Of course she could. It was pretty obvious he'd done nothing wrong. But then he'd expect answers to his questions, and she wasn't ready to give them. "I don't have an intense curiosity about you," she lied. She stood and picked up the full tray, which prevented her from running, but gave her an excuse to make a hasty exit. "Excuse me, I have work to do."

She staved off the annoying tears and went to the kitchen, where she set the tray on the worktable. She'd ask the cook to take food to Hank and see the dog had something to eat and fresh water. That way, she should manage to avoid them both until he left.

Milly was hanging her apron on the peg near the door and retrieving her coat and hat. The middle-aged cook gestured to the stove. "There's a stew prepared, fresh bread, and I've left a cake and made up some punch you can put with the champagne."

"You're leaving?"

"Don't you remember? You gave me a few days off so I could go visit my sister."

Jolie put her hand to her head. She never forgot important things like giving the cook time off, but it had slipped her mind while she'd been dwelling on Hank. Now he would become an even bigger distraction, because she would be the one looking after him instead. "I do remember now. Would you be able to get word to the Hardts that Mr. Donovan won't be attending dinner tonight?"

"I guess I can make a stop," Milly grumbled. "Should I tell them he's here?"

That would ruin his chances for sure if that crusading woman heard Hank was staying at the whorehouse she wanted to close down.

"No! Just say his dog is injured and he's indisposed."

Milly nodded and pulled the kitchen door shut firmly behind her as she left.

Jolie lifted the lid to the Dutch oven and inhaled the delicious aroma. The stew could be shared with Hank, but the cake and fortified punch were intended for the customers, along with the plentiful liquor.

She carried the cake on a platter into the front parlor. Angelique and Felice were setting up chairs along one wall, clearing the floor for dancing. There was no sign of the new girl, and their piano player wasn't at his usual spot. "Where's Milton?"

"He's sick," Felice lamented.

No music? That would put a damper on the evening.

"What happened to Belle?"

Felice shrugged. "Who knows? She's like a ghost. We never see her except late at night."

Belle remained something of a mystery. She kept to herself and ate at different times than the others and didn't socialize much. On the other hand, she possessed an exotic beauty some men clamored for, so she had made a good addition to the house. Jolie guessed the girl was at least part Chinese, although she claimed to be French and used a fake French name, like the other girls. Men paid more for French women under the false impression they were less inhibited and more talented. Both were skills that could be taught.

Jolie set the cake platter on the serving table. "I'll tell her she's expected in the parlor."

"No need. I'm here." The tiny woman entered the room, giving Jolie a brief glance, before training her eyes to the floor. Her straight black hair flowed loose down her back, and she wore a bright red silk gown that complimented her translucent complexion and golden-brown eyes. She was easily the prettiest of the girls, but she wasn't the best dancer. Felice held that honor. Angelique ended up with men who liked to hear themselves talk.

Jolie surveyed the formal parlor. The gas lamps cast a warm glow over the room, and bottles of champagne had been tucked into buckets of ice. The girls could mix any stronger drinks the men requested. Now if only they had music...

A knock sounded at the front door, and Jolie consulted the watch pinned to her bodice. It wasn't even half-past five. "The miners are early."

"What a surprise," Felice replied dryly. "I'll get the punch."

Jolie went to the front door and welcomed the three men into the hallway, all repeat customers who paid in gold....the best kind.

"Good evening Johnny, Ned..." The two blue-eyed charmers loved to dance and drink, and they always tipped well. "Hello, Bud." This one, on the other hand, was an intolerable braggart who had a problem controlling his pinching fingers. She'd come within inches of refusing him entry after his "playful" pinches had left bruises on Angelique's tender skin.

Jolie eyed the gun in a holster on Bud's hip and held out her hand. "No firearms allowed inside. I'll lock it up until you leave."

He grumbled as he put the heavy revolver into her palm. "Don't seem right a man can't keep his protection handy."

"No one here poses any danger to you." She smiled at the three men as they turned into the parlor. "Have fun and mind your manners."

"We will," the brothers chimed.

Bud simply smirked and walked past without another word.

What a contrast to Hank's polite and pleasant smile. Why couldn't more men be like Hank? That was easy to answer; he was a one of a kind. There weren't any other men like him, or if there were, she'd never had the pleasure of meeting them.

Hank approached life with an appealing mixture of optimism and determination. He didn't complain about how good others had it, or whine about how he deserved better, even though in her opinion, he did. She was glad she'd been here when he needed help. Possibly, he'd be able to do her a small favor in return.

Jolie checked her watch again and addressed Angelique. "Go ahead and serve the men drinks, while I try to round up a piano player."

In the back parlor, the lights were still burning. Hank had remained on the floor, although he'd stretched out his legs and leaned his shoulders against the settee, with one hand resting on the dog's shoulder. He had his eyes closed, but as she came into the room, he opened them.

"I'm sorry I woke you."

"I wasn't sleeping."

Well if that was true, she didn't feel so bad about asking, "Do you know how to play the piano?"

His brow creased in puzzled amusement. "Are you offering me a job?"

If only it were that easy to keep him with her.

"Our piano player is sick. We generally having dancing for the first hour, but none of us know how to play."

"I can plunk out a few tunes." Hank drew his foot back and hooked his elbows on the settee behind him for leverage, then stood up. "Bear's been snoring. I suspect he'll sleep a little while longer."

"We'll only need you for an hour. After that, I can get you something to eat." She smiled fondly at the snoring dog.

"If he wakes up, I'm sure we can find something for him too."

She gave Hank her arm and guided him to the front of the house. As they entered the front parlor, the three miners, already seated with girls on their laps, looked up. Three pairs of eyes widened.

"What the hell is *he* doin' here?" Bud demanded.

Hank's grip on her arm tightened and Jolie frowned, annoyed by what she assumed was the bully's disdain for Hank's blindness. "Mr. Donovan has agreed to play the piano for us."

"Where's the dog?" Ned eyed Hank fearfully.

Apprehension tickled Jolie's spine. *Oh no, it couldn't be...* But the hard set of Hank's jaw confirmed her suspicion. These men had been involved in the altercation, and one of them had shot Bear.

"I hope the cussed thing is dead," Bud sneered. "Damn dog attacked a woman."

With a look of alarm, Angelique left the man's lap. She seemed more scared of Bud than the possibility the dog posed any danger.

"Bear didn't attack anyone," Hank ground out. "I was pushed into that hysterical woman, and my dog put himself between us to keep me from falling. If you hadn't encouraged your friend to take hold of his leash, Bear wouldn't have growled. He wouldn't have done anything further unless I told him to attack."

Bud came to his feet with his hands fisted. "You callin' me a liar?"

Felice cast a silent appeal with her eyes toward Jolie. Yes, the situation was unraveling fast. Thankfully, the angry miner didn't have his gun. But if he went after Hank with his fists, as it seemed he was itching to do, Hank would be at a disadvantage and outnumbered. Jolie made a quick decision. She would send these other men home and let everyone cool off.

"Gentlemen, I think our evening has come to an end."

Felice and Belle took her cue and went quickly to the other side of the room to join Angelique.

Johnny got up and threw a disgusted look at his brother. "Dang it, Ned, I told you to stay away from that dog. Now we're missing out on a good time."

"Well I didn't know *he* worked here," Ned replied, gesturing at Hank.

"You can't throw us out!" Bud roared. "We got a right to be here, same as him." The brawny miner took a threatening step in Jolie's direction.

Jolie dropped Hank's arm, drew up her skirts, and calmly removed the derringer she kept tucked into her garter, which halted the miner in his tracks. She took great pleasure in seeing his face turn red. "Time to leave, Mr. Nance."

Bud veered toward the exit of the room, where Jolie and Hank still stood. On his way out, he turned and pointed a finger in her direction. "I'll come back and take care of you, you uppity whore. Right after I take care of that blind sonofabitch."

Hank's hand shot out and grabbed the other man by the coat, jerking him around, then threw a punch so fast Jolie had no time to react. Bud staggered backwards, hitting the doorframe, as blood began spurting from his nose.

Jolie's jaw dropped. How the devil had Hank struck a bull's-eye?

With a snarl, Hank stretched out his hands and went after his tormentor, letting loose an unearthly roar of rage that was downright menacing.

Bud whirled around and fled out the front door; Ned and Jack followed fast on his heels.

Jolie caught hold of Hank's coat before he made it outside, knowing he wouldn't see the step and would fall flat on his face. "Hold on, Lancelot. You need your horse."

"I *need* to get my hands around that sorry son-of-a-gun's neck. If he comes after you, I swear I'll kill him." Hank's flushed complexion, and the fury burning in his eyes, made it clear he was dead serious.

The thought of him going after those belly-crawlers scared her to death. She gripped his arms to hold him in place. "Don't even think about challenging them. They won't fight fair. In the morning when it's light, we can go to Sheriff Draven and report them for shooting your dog, and we'll tell him about the threats. I'll bet he makes them leave town. He doesn't like troublemakers."

Looking somber, Hank lifted his hands to her shoulders. She sensed he was about the pull her into his arms and forced herself to step backwards, away from him. It was the last thing she wanted to do, but to avoid being hurt, she had to keep her distance, physically and emotionally.

His high color faded to dull stains below his cheekbones. "I've messed things up for you, haven't I? Those were your customers, and I drove them away."

In fact, a whole evening's earnings had gone out that door. But more would've been lost had a fight broken out.

"Don't waste your time feeling sorry for something you didn't cause. Who needs customers like them?" she scoffed. "Plenty of other men would love to take their place. Why, I could snap my fingers and they'd come running."

"Yeah, I bet they would." Hank flexed his fingers, fisting them, looking none too pleased.

He knew where he was, right? What business she was

in? She'd seen customers become jealous when they formed an attachment to a particular girl, but she was sure Hank's reaction had more to do with Bud's threats. He hadn't formed an attachment to *her* of course. It wouldn't be good for either of them, and it wasn't what she wanted. No, of course not.

So why was her heart beating faster at the mere thought?

CHAPTER 8

*L*ater that night, Hank woke to rattling sounds coming from the kitchen and Bear's low growls. He rolled over, got to his knees, and put his hand on the dog's head. "Shhh."

If one of the girls had gotten up, he didn't want Bear to scare her.

"Maybe someone's looking for food," he whispered.

Earlier, Jolie had brought them a hearty loaf of bread and savory stew. There were scraps from the girls' meals for Bear, along with a bowl of fresh water. She'd given Hank a glass of wine. He'd thanked her—again—when what he'd really wanted to do was take her in his arms and kiss her. She'd left before he could work up the nerve to try.

The rattling sounds started up again.

Hank tensed. Should he go check it out? Bear had been up and walking a bit earlier, but the dog wasn't in any condition to confront an intruder. On the other hand, they couldn't just sit here, waiting for those men to come back and exact their revenge.

A soft scuffling came from the hall, which almost sounded like someone sliding slippers on the wood floor. Whoever it was stopped at the doorway. Then a flickering light pierced the darkness. "Hank?"

He relaxed, hearing Jolie's whisper. "Yeah, I'm awake. Was that you in the kitchen?"

"I couldn't sleep so I came down for a piece of cake. I thought you might want some too." The small light came closer and he decided it had to be a candle. He couldn't make out much more. His vision was terrible in the day, but even worse at night.

"I'll put this tray here." She set it on a low table in front of him. "How's Bear?"

"Better. After he ate, he got up and I took him out. I had to go out too."

"I hope you were careful."

"Always."

Jolie sat down on the floor next to him, close enough Hank could breathe in her sweet scent. "Milly made a black walnut cake. It's my favorite."

"I prefer orange blossom."

"Is that a type of cake?" she asked in a wry tone.

"It's sweet and tempting, better than cake, I'd wager." He really shouldn't be flirting, but he couldn't resist.

"Would you like some of this cake?"

"Certainly, if you'll show me where it is."

She lifted then guided his hand so he could find the plate. "Here's a fork."

"I'll just use my fingers. Otherwise, I'll be wearing Milly's cake," he explained genially before he took a bite. The gooey icing stuck to his fingers and lips, and after he'd licked them, she gave him a napkin. She met his special needs without making him feel awkward about having them. "Thank you. That was delicious."

"You're welcome. I didn't think about how difficult it might be for you to use a fork." Jolie took the plate and it clattered as she set it aside. "You inspire me, Hank."

"With my cake eating skills?" he joked.

"Impressive, but no."

He couldn't think of an amusing retort, because he was so surprised at her compliment, particularly after he'd ruined her plans for the evening. In fact, he was surprised she'd sat down on the floor next to him rather than taking a chair.

"I was just thinking about how brave you are." She stunned him again with another tribute. He assumed she was referring to his crazy attack on that bully. Fortunately, she'd stopped him before he got himself killed.

"Are you talking about when I went after Bud? I was sure you thought I'd lost my mind."

"Only for a moment." He could hear a smile in her voice. "I do admire your determination to protect me, also, your devotion to Bear, and the fact that you came out here on your own. I can't imagine how it must be to struggle with finding your way around a place you're familiar with, much less somewhere entirely new."

Jolie had left her warm bed to come down to feed him cake and heap praises on his head? He must be dreaming. If he was, he hoped he wouldn't wake up.

He'd been restless earlier, worrying that she would want him gone before morning, wishing he'd handled things differently, and wondering how he could make it up to her. "As long as we're handing out compliments, may I say I admire your courage?"

"It's easy to be courageous when you have a derringer tucked into your garter."

"I'll have to remember that the next time I put on my garters."

She laughed and bumped against him. As Hank laughed with her, he put his arm around her. When she didn't resist, he snuggled her closer, and she fit into his arms like she'd been made for him. Feeling more confident, he toyed with a wealth of soft curls flowing over her arms. She'd come to him with her hair down. The thought accelerated his heartbeat. Reaching over, he touched thin, silky fabric. Her robe? He found her clavicle with his fingertips and followed it to the soft dip at the base of her throat, where he felt her swallow.

"What are you doing, Hank?" she whispered.

"Looking at you."

"With your fingers?"

"That's how I can see you best." He knew he was playing with fire, but he couldn't help it. She'd been kind and generous, even flirtatious, but that didn't mean he should be holding her and touching her like a lover. He knew full well what he ought *not* to be doing. He did it anyway.

He shifted his hip and turned toward her, found her cheek with one hand, and brought his mouth closer to where he approximated hers would be. Her rapid breathing helped him find her lips, which parted beneath his.

She sighed and put her hands to his chest. Hank recalled her earlier admonition about kissing not being part of the *service*. But instead of pushing him away, she gripped his lapels and pulled him closer. Elated, he deepened the kiss. Did the fact she encouraged him mean she wasn't just providing a service, but wanted him as desperately as he wanted her?

Something had happened tonight when he'd come face-to-face with her reality. He'd been gripped by a fierce rage, and not just because those men had shot his dog. He longed to spirit Jolie away from this place, away from her sordid life, and shower her with real affection. Not the kind that came from a financial exchange. He couldn't stand thinking of her with other men. He wanted her for himself. It was that simple.

Who was he kidding? Nothing about this was simple. The desire, the emotions, everything all knotted up in his chest, was complicated as hell.

Jolie found it increasingly hard to breathe normally while Hank was kissing her. Sleep had eluded her, and getting the cake had just been an excuse to check on him. But she hadn't meant to stay for very long, certainly not long enough for this to happen. The moment he'd touched her, her willpower had evaporated.

Shivers raced across her skin and her toes curled against the carpet. She ran her fingers across his strong jaw. Bristly and rumpled was a good look on him. She combed her fingers through his hair and lost herself in the delicious intimacy.

The way he cupped her cheek, with such tenderness, and brushed his lips over hers, back and forth, tempted her to become an active participant, not just a willing one. For a man who'd suffered, as he must have, he'd retained a surprising sweetness, which drew her like a bee to a flower.

For some reason, Hank hadn't let her pleasure him the day before. But now, he acted as if he was intent on providing pleasure, only his kisses evoked more than just a passionate response.

Jolie trembled at the storm of emotions sweeping over and through her, tearing down walls she'd spent years constructing for her own protection. How easily he was able to arouse her absolutely terrified her. She planted her hands on his chest and turned her face away, ending their kiss. "Hank, why are you doing this?"

He trailed kisses across her cheek. "I want to show you what real affection feels like."

His plea squeezed her heart. She'd be a fool to let herself fall for Hank. Watching him walk away wouldn't be easy, and it was inevitable he would leave. One day he'd tire of her, or his wife would find out and put an end to it. A woman like Ophelia Rathbone would not look the other way.

"I know all about real affection." She didn't intend to say more, but the pathetic story just poured out of her. "I was in love and stupid enough to think he loved me in return. When he left to search for gold, I followed him out here only to find that he'd already set up house with another woman. Then he had the audacity to die in a mining accident. The same week, I lost the baby I was carrying."

Jolie turned slightly away from him and buried her face in her hands. The memories had dredged up emotions she'd thought were long dead. She couldn't keep the secrets in any longer. If she could let them out, maybe she would finally stop hurting.

"I couldn't go home and face my family, and I had nowhere else to go. One of the miners offered me money in exchange for my *affection*." She shuddered as the past barreled through her mind. "Not only did I take money from that man, I sold myself to two of his friends so I would have enough to buy food. After that, it just seemed the only way to survive. So I know what real affection feels like. You can keep it."

He laid his hand on her shoulder, but she shrugged it off. She had to get out of here or she'd soon be right back in his arms.

"Jolie, don't go." Groping, he caught her wrist. "I won't force myself on you."

His willpower wasn't the problem.

"You weren't forcing me to do anything. I let you kiss me, but we both know this is going nowhere. If you need release, I can—" No, she was too vulnerable right now. "I'll call down one of the girls and they can take you upstairs."

"I'm not interested in them." He circled his thumb over the back of her hand, a tender gesture. She couldn't recall ever being touched with such care. Not even the man she once thought had loved her had been so gentle.

Tears stung her eyes and she tugged at her wrist, growing desperate to get away before she broke down and wept.

He loosened his hold enough for her to pull away. "Don't be afraid."

If he could detect her fear, soon enough he would figure out the reason, and that would give him too much power over her. She lifted her chin and hardened her voice. "I'm not afraid."

Light cast by the candle bathed the side of his face and revealed the slight lift on one side of his mouth, a wry smile, which said he wasn't fooled a bit. "Considering what you went through, I don't blame you for not trusting me. Self-protection is a powerful instinct. I understand more than you realize."

"What is it you think you understand?"

"Loss."

His one-word answer cut through her weak defense and went straight through her heart. She'd told him earlier she wasn't interested in knowing more about him, but that had been a lie too. Her infatuation fed an intense curiosity.

"Do you mean the loss of your sight?

"No, although that's part of it. Seven years ago, I was traveling by steamboat from St. Louis to Memphis to marry the woman I thought I would live with for the rest of my life. My father and I were sitting on the top deck talking about my recent acceptance into medical school. I remember the last thing he said to me. He'd taught me all he knew, and told me I needed to learn new things so I could come back and teach him.

"There was an explosion—the boilers blew is what they told me later. The blast threw me clear out of the boat, the force knocked me unconscious, and I landed on the shore. They found me in the grass. My father wasn't so lucky.

"When I woke up, I couldn't see clearly. I could distinguish light and darkness, and make out shapes, but everything was muddy and blurred. The doctors told me the force of the blow must've caused bleeding or some kind of damage inside my eyes. They thought if I gave it time, my vision might improve. I held out hope for two years. Nothing changed."

Jolie could envision Hank as that young man: intelligent, educated, with his whole life planned and waiting for him, including a beautiful woman. In one cruel moment, he'd lost a beloved father, his sight and his future. She wiped away tears streaming down her face. "What about your bride?"

"She waited a few months to see if I would recover, then she cried off."

Selfish hag. She should've rushed to Hank's side. Jolie shook her head, disgusted, but not surprised, having seen that coming. "She didn't truly love you."

He nodded. "It seems we've both had bad luck when it comes to love."

They'd both been cheated out of more than that.

Jolie leaned forward and reached over to the low table to retrieve a napkin to dry her eyes. "Your misfortune went beyond losing the woman you loved. You had to give up your dream of becoming a doctor as well."

Hank drew up one knee, stretching the other leg out, and leaned his shoulders against the settee. He stared into the darkness with a reflective expression. "Actually, that was harder to let go of. I wasn't sure what to do. I'd lost myself."

Something else they had in common. That rash, innocent girl who thought love could conquer anything had been lost four years ago. "How did you find yourself again?"

"After my sister's husband died, she needed a way to support herself and her two children, so she started making greeting cards. I'd relied on her for two years, and I knew I needed to get out and help her. It was nearly impossible at first. I had to learn my way around, and for a time, to depend on my eight-year-old nephew to guide me. Then we found Bear."

The dog stirred at his name and moved closer, curling up at Hank's side. Hank stroked Bear's head as he continued, "He'd been beaten and starved, and it took us awhile to earn his trust. He eventually came around."

No doubt the result of Hank's patient determination.

"He started following me everywhere. Then I noticed he would nudge me away from furniture when I was about to fall over it. I thought if he was that smart, he might learn to look out for other obstacles, so I started working with him.

We've been together for five years. Haven't we boy?" Hank rubbed the dog's ears, and Bear licked his hand. "We take care of each other."

Jolie gazed wistfully at the affectionate exchange. "It's good to have a friend like that."

Hank turned his attention to her, and the smile he gave her seemed wistful. "If you had an opportunity to start over and begin a new life, would you take it?"

Was he suggesting she could leave her current life behind if the stars aligned just right? That rarely happened, and it certainly wouldn't happen for her. She refused to let him draw her into imagining *what if*.

Much as she might wish she and Hank could run away and be together—and he had proposed no such thing—it was only fanciful thinking. He had to marry a woman like Ophelia Rathbone to get what he wanted. He might be signaling he was willing to take a mistress, which in Jolie's mind was only trading one form of prostitution for another. If he couldn't understand how much she stood to lose with that arrangement, she wasn't going to enlighten him.

"Why would I want to start over? I've just become the madam here. I can finally afford a nice place to live, good food, fancy clothes, and since I'm running the business, I no longer have to take men upstairs unless I choose to."

"You chose to take me upstairs."

He *would* remind her...but she would remind him. "And you walked away."

He frowned at that. "You don't understand why?"

"Not really."

Hank grew serious, the look on his face appeared almost angry. "I don't want you to view me as a customer, because I don't think of you as a whore."

He *was* suggesting a fantasy. It would be funny, if it weren't so sad.

Jolie sighed to relieve the pressure in her chest. "But that's what I am, Hank. Don't forget it. Don't fool yourself into thinking I can be anything else."

CHAPTER 9

In the morning, Jolie got up and fixed a big breakfast for Hank and Bear. To her relief, the dog was up and moving around, and showing great interest in a bone she'd saved from the stew. Hank had tried to be helpful, but had ended up overturning the milk and she'd shooed him to the table. After they'd eaten, he attached Bear's harness and leash, then led the limping dog to the door.

Jolie set the dishes aside in the sink and hurried after them. "Are you sure Bear shouldn't stay off his feet for another day?"

Hank put his hand on her shoulder and smiled apologetically. "We've disrupted your life enough. We'll be fine back at my room. I'll make sure he rests for a couple days."

He withdrew his hand and the warmth she felt at his touch fled. She had to stop thinking about how warm and good it felt when he touched her. His presence had upended her routine enough. If she planned to remain madam at *La Maison*, she had to commit to what was best for the business.

Still, there was no reason she couldn't make sure Hank and Bear made it safely to the saloon. "Wait for me to dress and I'll walk with you, just in case."

Hank again turned before he'd reached the front door. "No need, we can go it alone."

Jolie took a step back. He might as well have said he was ashamed to be seen with her. "Oh. Of course. That would be best. I'll say goodbye then."

"Wait, Jolie." He caught her by the sleeve of her robe, so she had no choice but to stop, or surrender it to him. Then he took hold of her arm, drawing her to him, and gave her an unexpected hug.

"I only meant I don't want you to rearrange your morning any more that you already have on my account. I appreciate everything you've done, and I don't want to be more of a burden than I've already been."

She wrapped her arms around him, then thought better of it and stepped out of his embrace. It was best for both of them if they didn't continue to act like friends, which they couldn't be. "Goodbye then."

After a moment's hesitation, Hank lifted his hat to her and left.

Jolie watched from the door as he and Bear moved slowly across the porch past the hitching posts and into the slushy street. This cold couldn't be good for the dog's health. "You will send word to let me know how he's doing?" she called out.

Hank glanced back. "I will."

Jolie spun around and hurried upstairs to her bedroom. Everyone else was still asleep, but she couldn't go back to bed. For one, she couldn't get her mind off Hank long enough to shut it down.

From a table near the bed, she picked up the Valentine

card he'd given her and ran her fingers over the lace. She would treasure it forever, and he'd probably forget all about it, if he hadn't already.

She pulled out a drawer and slipped it inside. What she needed was a distraction...and she had one! Her business was under attack, and it was up to her to defend it. If those crusaders could start a petition, why, then she could go round up support for her own crusade—to keep *La Maison* open.

Going through her dresses in the wardrobe, she selected a green velvet gown and lifted it off the hook. Not exactly a day dress, but it looked good on her and might stir up some appreciation. The new publisher in town offered printing services. She could purchase leaflets and hand them out to the miners and the other men in the community who would rally behind her.

An hour later, she entered a new building that had recently become home to the newspaper office.

Joseph Hurst, Esquire, had arrived last month and had started the *Noelle Gazette*. The first thing she noticed was the strong smell of paper and ink, and then the mess. The small space was knee-deep in newsprint, with leaflets and posters scattered all over and stuffed into cubbyholes. In the back, a boy in an ink-stained apron ran the printer, producing clatter, and even more clutter.

Behind one of the stacks of newspapers, she found Mr. Hurst hunched over his desk, furiously scribbling. Smoke curled from the thick cigar firmly clenched between his teeth. She found it interesting that he had his spectacles pushed up onto the top of his head, instead of wearing them, as most people would do, to help him read.

"Excuse me, Mr. Hurst?"

"Yes, what is it?" he replied, without looking at her.

Had he seen her enter and decided she wasn't worth his time? Her money was as good as anyone else's.

"I would like to order some leaflets to be printed. A hundred should do."

He placed his pen back into the inkwell and looked up, as if he'd just taken notice of her. "A hundred leaflets. For what?"

Jolie stiffened at his rudeness. "Are you always this impolite to customers? If so, I'm surprised you remain in business."

The editor's intense gaze remained on her a moment longer, then he stood and made a slight, belated bow. She caught the spectacles as they fell off his head and handed them back to him.

He tucked them into his vest pocket without even a thank you. "What can I do for you, ma'am?"

Jolie considered offering him her name, then changed her mind. He hadn't bothered with introductions, so neither would she. "One hundred leaflets, Mr. Hurst. And I'll need help with the wording."

"We can write and print whatever you need."

"Good. How much will this cost?"

His gaze flickered over her. Not with interest, as she knew *that* look. It seemed more as if he were trying to place her. He wasn't a customer at *La Maison*, and they'd never met, so perhaps he didn't know who she was. If he surmised she was one of the local newlyweds, this made his boorish behavior all the more puzzling.

"Five dollars," he stated.

He must've recognized her after all. Or thought she printed her own money.

"That seems steep."

"Not for writing and printing both." He gestured at a

chair. "Have a seat."

She removed her cloak and draped it over the back of the chair when he didn't take it.

The editor had sat down and pulled over a clean sheaf of paper on the desk in front of him. "What is it you want to advertise?"

Jolie firmed her lips to keep from laughing. Oh, that was rich. How would he react if she listed the parlor house's available services? He seemed dour and unlikely to appreciate a joke. "I'd like to publish a petition, not an advertisement."

"What is the petition concerning?"

"Preserving *La Maison*...as a cultural treasure." She'd just come up with that, and thought it sounded pretty good.

Mr. Hurst leaned back in his chair. He didn't actually smile, but the stern expression shifted enough to imply amusement. "You want to publish a petition to preserve a whorehouse as a *cultural treasure*?"

"That's right. And you might put something in there about how it provides a necessary refuge for hard-working men, who have no home to go to after spending long days in the dark and cold. Do these good men not deserve a place where they can go to relax and find respite from their toils?"

The editor held out his pen. "Maybe you should write this. You're doing a better job than I could."

She'd been rehearsing what the petition might say, but she wasn't sure he couldn't add something more to spice it up. "Didn't you write the other petition being circulated by Mrs. Hammond and Miss Rathbone?"

Hurst withdrew the pen. "No. I learned about it from Mrs. Stiles and Mrs. Sharp. Seemed a thing I ought to be reporting."

Jolie sat up straight, surprised. 'The railroad officials'

wives told you about the petition? I assumed the two women named in the article had approached you."

"Mrs. Hammond and Miss Rathbone haven't been available for an interview," Hurst grumbled.

This certainly shed a new light on the situation. Jolie recalled Felicity and Ophelia hadn't mentioned the petition when challenged, and in fact, had talked about other things. It was possible—even probable—the older ladies had started it and were hiding behind the younger women's names to avoid a battle with their husbands. Dick and Sol certainly didn't support closing down the parlor house— they were two of *La Maison's* best customers. That didn't mean they'd publicly oppose the preacher's wife. Their jealous spouses had come up with a good scheme.

Jolie sat forward, holding the editor's gaze. "I spoke with Mrs. Hammond and Miss Rathbone, and they seem more concerned with addressing women's plights than starting petitions. I now question whether they even wrote the petition. You might've talked to them first to get your story straight."

Hurst set the pen aside, frowning at her. "They've been too busy with a slew of suitors vying for Miss Rathbone's hand."

A *slew* of suitors were after Ophelia? Jolie suppressed a flare of hope, but she tamped it down. That might not be good news for Hank, and it didn't necessarily mean good news for her either. He needed an acceptable bride, which she was not. Regardless, it didn't matter. What mattered was getting *her* petition written and circulated before the other one gained too much momentum.

She pasted on a polite smile. "Will you finish my petition and print the copies? I'll be back later today to collect them."

The editor leaned back and crossed his arms over this chest. "Won't be able to get to them that fast. We've got other orders."

He might not want to get to it at all. For all she knew, he supported the efforts to close down *La Maison*. He never stopped by, not like the previous newspaperman, Horatio, who'd been a regular. Mr. Hurst couldn't be more different from the pale, fussy man who'd worshiped tidiness and believed in the liberal usage of pomade. Hurst's unkempt mane curled over his collar, and he resembled a logger more than a newspaper editor. Aside from being rude, he looked like the type Felice would enjoy. Would he be amenable to helping them if she offered him a discount?

Jolie presented her card and made an introduction. "Miss Jolie LaFemme, proprietor of *La Maison*. I might be able to come up with an added incentive, *if* you could get to my job right away."

Mr. Hurst took the card between his first two fingers, as if considering the bribe. Then he dropped it onto the messy desk, much to her disappointment. "Five dollars is the charge and they won't be done until tomorrow...if you decide you still want them after today, that is."

"Why wouldn't I want them?"

"Have you looked at today's paper?" He reached out, picked up the newspaper, and handed it to her. On the front page was the headline: *More Brides For Noelle?*

Jolie breathed faster. *Oh no!* It was starting again! More brides, more wives...more women like Felicity Hammond and Ophelia Rathbone.

Jolie's gaze fell to the smaller type just beneath the headline, and she began to feel lightheaded.

Certain House Soon Put To Better Use

CHAPTER 10

*H*ank spent the weekend in his room over the Golden Nugget, nursing Bear back to health, and contemplating his future...without Jolie. He hadn't seen her since Friday, and he still needed to send word to ease her worries about Bear, as she'd asked, but it was time he stopped thinking there might be some future for them together.

Who could blame her for refusing to leave behind her hard-won position and relative security? He'd offered her nothing in return for his demands she treat him differently from other men. She didn't trust he was all that different. She'd been betrayed, broken, and in all likelihood, abused. And the losses she'd suffered—first her lover, then a baby? God, it broke his heart to imagine how alone and scared she must've been.

Though she'd never admit it, she craved true affection, which he longed to give her. But choosing Jolie meant giving up his pursuit for acceptance in the community, and his dream of becoming an investor in what was being hailed as Colorado's biggest silver mine. If he lost this chance, he still couldn't give Jolie a nice home and fancy clothes. He could give her another Valentine card. She needed security, not sentimentality.

He scrubbed his fingers through his hair, and downed the whiskey he'd ordered along with his breakfast, then got up from his table near the window. Once more, he'd let his heart get ahead of his good sense. He shouldn't forget what Jolie had told him. She had made her choice, just as he had to make his.

After cleaning up at the washbasin, brushing his teeth, and running a comb through his hair, he put on his best suit. His family depended on him. Once he'd married and gotten settled, he could send for Maggie, Davy and Kathleen. They'd all be together, and he would be content.

"C'mon boy," Hank called to Bear.

The dog jumped from the bed to the floor and his nails ticked on the planks as he trotted over to the door. Hank had been faithfully changing Bear's bandages, which could stay off the next day. The stitches would be removed in another week.

"That healing salve Mr. Hardt sent over worked wonders. You aren't even limping." Hank attached the dog's leash and rubbed Bear's ears. "Let's go find out if Miss Rathbone is still single."

Hank made his way downstairs with Bear in the lead. The noise coming from the saloon sounded like an army of honking geese or braying donkeys. As he passed through the darkened doorway and into the lighter room, the noise got even louder.

Bagpipes.

He'd never learned how to play them, but he was certain he could do better.

Oddly enough, people were clapping, and some jeered

with equal fervor. The saloon appeared as a moving sea, which meant it must be packed with people. Another scent mingled with the odors of whiskey and smoke. *Perfume.* There were ladies present.

A large, blurred figure appeared close within Hank's line of vision. "Mr. Donovan? Hank? Would you care to sit with us?"

Hank recognized the deep voice. "Culver?"

"That's right. My wife, Zee, is over there at our table. We'd be honored if you'd join us. You can meet our little Jem. She's about done with all this noise."

"What's going on?"

"The town is holding a talent show in honor of Lincoln's birthday. They even built a stage for the occasion. The winner gets a hundred dollars in gold."

"Holy smokes. I'll play the bagpipes for that kind of money. Come to think of it, I probably shouldn't or I won't win the prize for sure. But I could have Bear perform. Do we still have a chance to enter?" Hank doubted it, considering how poor his timing had been of late.

"Don't see why not. I'm announcing the acts. Come with me; I'll introduce you after these fellows are done with their screeching."

Hank instructed Bear to follow, and as they passed tables, he heard his name called.

"Hank Donovan! Good to see you! Your cards are selling out."

That would be Liam, the shopkeeper. Hank lifted his hand and looked in the direction where the voice had come from amidst the dark sea. "Great news, Mr. Fulton."

"Morning, Hank. Glad to see your dog is up and around."

The drawled greeting came from his left and Hank

recognized the Texas accent. He was closer to this table and could make out the speaker had stood, and when he put out his hand, Hardt shook it.

"Thank you, Mr. Hardt. That salve you sent did wonders."

"Woody made it. You two need to meet sometime."

"I'll make it a point."

Culver was on the move, so Hank waved at the mine owner. "I'll be back to talk to you after the talent show concludes."

"Good. I'll introduce you to the folks at our table."

Was one of them Ophelia?

Hank made a mental note of where the table was located, and continued on after Culver. The bagpipe players had ceased their clamor, and the crowd was giving them a weak ovation. Bear's howling would be an improvement over the previous performance.

"This here's our table, right up front," Culver said. "Looks like you have a chance to go onstage if you want. I'll make the announcement."

Go onstage...

Hank hesitated. A hundred dollars in gold was a lot of money, and he could add it to his investment. On the other hand, there was a very good possibility he'd make a complete fool of himself in front of the whole town. However, he'd never gotten anywhere worrying about embarrassment. *Carpe diem.*

He leaned toward Culver and said in a lowered voice, "Is Miss Rathbone sitting at Mr. Hardt's table?"

"Looks like her."

If he could think of a way to get Bear to retrieve something from her, it might amuse her and give them something to talk about later. "Do you have a stick or something my dog might fetch?"

"How about a baby rattle?"

"That'll do." Hank took the rattle and let the dog smell it. "Toy."

Bear loved toys, and he'd do anything to get someone to play with him.

"Will you take this to Miss Rathbone's table?" he asked Culver, handing back the rattle.

Culver chuckled. "Sure thing."

Hank introduced himself to Culver's wife and made small talk until the deed had been accomplished. When Culver returned, Hank followed him two steps up onto a stage. Gasps came from some of the tables up front. His big dog certainly had that effect on people. More than a few folks had said Bear was ugly, but Jolie had called him *beautiful*. That had endeared Hank to her faster than any greeting she could've given him.

Culver cleared his throat. "Ladies and gentlemen, welcome Hank Donovan and his amazing Bear!"

That sounded impressive. Now if he could just live up to the promotion. The clapping wasn't nearly as enthusiastic as it had been even for the bagpipes. At least there were no jeers.

Hank lifted his hands and the crowd grew silent. First, he would establish a few things that might help him avoid any misunderstandings and keep them both out of trouble.

"Good afternoon, everyone. As Mr. Daniels said, I'm Hank Donovan, and this is my dog, Bear. We've been working together for five years. I say working, because Bear has a job. He acts as my eyes. That's why he goes everywhere with me." Hank put his hand on the big dog's head. "He may look fierce, but he's very friendly...as long you're friendly."

The last line got a few chuckles.

"Seriously, folks. Bear won't hurt you. As part of this performance, I'm going to send him out into the audience to retrieve a toy, and then ask the person who has it to come up here and help me with a few tricks."

This time the clapping was louder.

"Miss Rathbone?" he called out. "Would you stand and hold up the object Mr. Daniels gave you? Once you're standing, please let me know."

Murmurs rippled through the crowd. A few men snickered. It seemed Miss Rathbone was taking her time about getting out of her seat. He hoped she wasn't shy about being in the spotlight.

"Miss Rathbone? Are you standing?"

"What? Oh, I'm sorry. What is it you want?" Her voice sounded pleasant enough, but she apparently had been woolgathering. Was she a daydreamer, or just bored already with his performance?

Hank spoke over the titters. "Do you have the baby rattle Mr. Daniels gave you?"

"A baby rattle?"

More guffaws.

Was she being difficult on purpose? He'd give her the benefit of not being very bright.

Hank held onto a polite smile. "I believe Mr. Daniels brought the item to you a few minutes ago."

"Yes, there is a rattle on the table."

"Would you pick it up? I'd like to send my dog to fetch it."

"Your dog?" She sounded doubtful.

"Yes. He'll be gentle."

"Very well."

"Fetch the toy." Hank instructed Bear and released the

leash. The dog bounded off the stage. After a few squeals, people began laughing.

From where Hank stood, he could see the occasional glowing light from what he surmised were candles at the edge of the stage. Good thing Bear hadn't knocked one over and started a fire. That would assure Hank of one thing— being ridden out of town on a rail, coated with tar and feathers.

"Shouldn't he be returning the rattle?" Ophelia called out.

Hank's heart gave a hiccup. Now wasn't a good time for Bear to misbehave. He brought up his hand and shielded his eyes, then dropped his arm. What was the use pretending he could see? Everyone was already starting to laugh at him. "What's he doing?" he called out.

"He appears to be taking it outside," Ophelia answered.

The laughter got even louder.

"Bear, come!" Hank commanded, and under his breath added, "And while you're at it, stop embarrassing me."

A moment later, he heard a commotion.

"He's bringing you a toy!" a man shouted with amusement.

"Got her by the skirts!" declared another.

Good God.

"Miss Rathbone, don't be concerned, just come along with him. He must think I wanted him to fetch you too."

"The dog isn't bringing you Miss Rathbone," a deep voice boomed. Something in the man's tone warned Hank the speaker wasn't enjoying the performance nearly as much as the rest of the crowd.

Bear's toenails clicked as he came onto the stage with someone in his wake. Small, light foot footsteps...who the...?

"Hello, Hank. That's quite a trick you taught him."

Poor Hank had turned a deep shade of red, which wasn't particularly flattering with his light complexion. "Jolie? Where did you—?"

"Come from? I was just coming over to peek in on the talent show." She didn't voice the truth, that she could care less about the community event. No one wanted a local madam showing up anyway. She'd actually been on her way over to check on him because she hadn't seen or heard from him, and had gotten worried something might've happened to his dog.

"Lo and behold, here came Bear with a baby rattle." She held up the item, which had the dog's slobber all over it, and the crowd broke into laughter.

Humor was the only thing that would save this performance.

"He gave me the rattle, then he took hold of my skirt and wanted me to come with him." She hadn't expected the dog to do that, but she'd gone rather than risk having her skirt torn. Not only that, she'd realized she needed to rescue Hank from the embarrassing situation he'd somehow gotten himself into.

She'd heard him call on Ophelia Rathbone, and had seen the other woman stand. Then she'd abruptly sat back down when the man next to her glared as if he wanted to storm the stage and strangle Hank. The dog hadn't paid the other woman any mind after retrieving the rattle. Perhaps the man had glared at Bear too. The stranger had gripped the back of her chair. He couldn't have been more obvious: Ophelia was off the market. Hank just didn't know it yet.

But no one was paying a lick of attention to Ophelia and her surly suitor. All eyes were now on the stage. The big dog had taken his place next to Hank and gazed at his master like he expected to be rewarded.

Jolie resisted the urge to lick her lips, which the crowd might misinterpret, and wouldn't help matters. The dog's antics could prove to be detrimental to Hank's future if people got the wrong idea. "I'm not sure why Bear came after me."

"He must like that pretty dress you're wearing, and wanted to borrow it." Hank's witty retort garnered a round of laughter.

She held out the drab wool skirt she'd chosen as her go-to-town outfit so she wouldn't draw unnecessary attention. "You think this dress is pretty?"

"What do you think Bear?" Hank asked the dog.

Bear barked.

People began to clap.

"Looks like you're a hit," she said under the noise. "Do you have another trick?"

"Are you kidding? He's the one coming up with them," Hank replied, loud enough for only her to hear. He then turned to Bear and spoke loud enough the crowd could hear. "And you! You ought to *beg* her pardon for bringing her up here and embarrassing her." Hank swept his hand upward, and Bear immediately sat back on his haunches and lifted his front paws like a supplicant.

Hank gave an exaggerated nod. "I'm surprised you're not *hiding* in shame for soiling her skirt."

Bear dropped flat and crossed his paws over his muzzle, peeking up at them as if to ask whether he was doing it right.

The crowd loved it. Jolie actually began to enjoy getting into the act as well.

"Nonsense," she said with a sniff. "He's a perfect

gentleman. He only tried to take my hand." She held it out. "Or maybe he meant to *shake* my hand?"

Bear came up into a sitting position and raised one paw, much to the delight of the audience. She suspected he would know how to do that, but he made it look as if they'd been practicing together for years.

She took his paw and smiled. "See? Everyone approves of Bear."

"Hmm, looks like he found a new partner. I'm not sure I'm needed." With a mock frown, Hank started toward the stairs as if he intended to leave. The dog raced over and blocked his path. When he stepped too near the lanterns lined up to provide light, Bear got in front of him and nudged him away, whining softly.

"You want me to stay up here?"

Bear pushed his head beneath Hank's hand and helped his master find the leash.

Hank grasped it, then shrugged. "I guess he's decided to keep me."

Laughing, Jolie clapped loudly, and the audience joined her. She stepped forward with a smile and grasped Hank's hand. "Think we need to take a bow?"

"Why not?"

Hank motioned to Bear, and the dog also put his head down, taking his bow, garnering the most applause.

Jolie followed Hank off the stage. As her euphoria faded, she noticed people were still staring at them. The small bubble of discomfort suddenly burst into a desperate urge to escape. She headed straight for the door, dodging men, and avoiding meeting the eyes of anyone in the crowd, especially the women. They must wonder why she'd shown up in the first place.

There had really been no need to rescue Hank. In catlike fashion, he would have landed on his feet and would've done just fine without her. Bear apparently hadn't thought so, but who could know what went on in a dog's mind?

She hurried down the boardwalk, her spool heels clacking on the boards. Seamus must've shoveled the snow and swept in preparation for the talent show. A faint sound of applause came from behind her. Perhaps it was another act, or maybe Hank was doing a reprise with Bear. His newfound popularity would help him win a bride when the next wagonload arrived and they took over *La Maison*.

She'd be out in the street along with Angelique, Felice and Belle. The only one she really worried about was Angelique. But they would all have to start over. It wasn't fair, damn it. It wasn't *fair!* They'd worked as hard as these men.

"Jolie!"

What did Pearl want?

Long strands of honey blonde hair escaped as Pearl's hood fell back when she dashed across the street, dodging a wagon loaded with mining supplies. She shouted an apology at the driver, whose scowl vanished, and was quickly replaced by a dreamy smile.

Jolie harrumphed. If it had been she who'd cut in front of him, he would've run her over and spit on her broken body. Pearl—whose beauty had inspired miners to pen poetry—could charm a vulture. No wonder Draven had fallen in love with her.

Pearl flipped her hood back over her head. "Brrr, it's cold out here."

"If you don't have your hood pulled up, I suppose it is."

"It *never* stays up."

Jolie couldn't resist the double entendre. "Did you come over here to lament your husband's marital difficulties?"

Her friend flashed a smile. "Draven has no such difficulty, if you really want to know."

"I really don't."

"Then let me tell you about my conversation with Mrs. Hardt."

"*Mrs.* Hardt?" Jolie's amusement vanished. "I thought Draven might appeal to *Mr.* Hardt. Why did you go to his wife? She despises us."

"That's not true. She cares very much. She and Mrs. Kinnison want to give the women of *La Maison* a better life, better opportunities."

"Before or after they kick us out?" Jolie dug into the pocket of her cloak. "Here, take a few of these flyers I had made up. I've been handing them around."

The single men had taken them and asked for extra favors for passing them out. She didn't bother approaching the married men.

Pearl took a handful and sighed. She might help, or not. It wasn't really her problem any longer. "Mrs. Hardt wouldn't kick you out of your home. I heard her warning Felicity not to get embroiled in this fight."

Jolie snorted in disgust. "Too late. Gertrude Stiles and that other hatchet face are determined to run us out of town. Other women are right there with them. They don't care about us."

Pearl grasped her arm. "Jolie, listen to me! Some of them *do* care. You don't have to leave, even if they do close *La Maison*. What Mrs. Hardt and Mrs. Kinnison will be doing with the mission is a true gift."

If there was one thing Jolie had learned, it was that a *gift* always had a catch. Except for that Valentine card. She still owed Hank for that, and it annoyed her to be in his debt.

"What kind of gift?" she asked.

"An opportunity to make a match."

"Oh good Lord." Jolie rolled her eyes. "I can imagine the kind of husbands we'd end up with—cheaters, thieves and lazy brutes, the kind of men who proposition us every other day. Who needs an introduction?"

"That's not at all what they're proposing. Mrs. Kinnison, if you recall, brought the first group of brides out here. They were all from the mission in Denver that serves women in unfortunate circumstances."

"Ah. You mean women like Felicity Hammond, whose father owns half of Denver, and aristocrats like Minnie Gold."

Pearl heaved an aggrieved sigh. "Felicity and Minnie were in unhappy situations."

"Pardon me if my heart doesn't bleed for them."

"Will you please stop being sarcastic and close-minded?"

"I don't know how else to be," Jolie said, this time with complete seriousness. She didn't have Pearl's natural beauty on the outside, or the inside. Although being around Hank *had* softened her heart...or maybe it was her head that was going soft.

"Why don't you talk to Felicity and Ophelia? See what they really want. I could arrange a meeting."

"Oh, I've already spoken with them. I can't imagine there's anything else they have to say to me." Jolie immediately felt guilty for dousing her friend's determined optimism. Sweet Pearl meant well, but she'd been one of the lucky few who'd gotten out of the business through a good marriage. Boum Boum had run off with that miner, Orvis, but who knew where they were, or if they'd even stayed together. Most women who started down this path wouldn't escape unless they left in a pine box.

"You really believe we could find good husbands?" Jolie asked, softening her tone.

"I found Draven."

"Wasn't that his idea?"

"Actually, it was Reverend Hammond's idea to have us pretend marriage. We just made it official."

"And now you live in a room next to the jail."

"He's promised to build us a cabin...as we add children." Pearl's hand came to rest on her flat stomach, and a smile curved her lips.

"A baby?" Jolie choked out. The one thing she wanted most and would never have. "How did— But you never were — I don't understand."

Pearl shook her head with obvious amazement. "I'm not sure I do either. I didn't expect I could conceive, but somehow it happened."

"Hmm, I don't believe in miracles." Jolie did believe Pearl was more deserving of Divine mercy. "It just sounds like marriage agrees with you."

"Yes it does. You should try it."

Jolie dipped her chin and blinked fast to stop the tears. She wouldn't get the chance, because she wouldn't take the chance. Hank had been right in saying she was afraid. But why should she let her heart be ripped out again? Besides, Hank needed a respectable wife, and he hadn't asked her to marry him at any rate.

She forced a laugh. "Oh, you know me. I'm too bossy to be married, and I'm way too busy to be waiting on some man hand and foot."

Pearl's cheerful expression faded into one she didn't wear very often. Sadness. "You need to think about what you'll do if the town votes to close down the house."

The possibility struck dread in Jolie's heart. She raised her chin in defiance. "I'll find another place to work."

"You could find something more lasting," Pearl suggested softly.

Hank had made a rather indirect offer. He'd asked her if she'd ever leave her job, and had said he didn't want her to view him as a customer. Which implied he might support her as a mistress. She'd rather be Hank's mistress than some other man's wife.

Such a relationship might work for her, but for him it could prove to be disastrous, especially with the married women out crusading against sin. She was already among the damned, and her life had been ruined years ago. Hank had a chance for something so much better. In refusing him, she had done the right thing.

"I've made my bed, so to speak, and that's where I'll continue to sleep."

CHAPTER 11

*E*arly on Valentine's Day morning, Hank dressed in his best suit and set out for a meeting Charlie Hardt had set up. Not wanting to be late, Hank polished off a quick breakfast and headed out before most people in town were awake. The only sounds came from the direction of the mine, where they started work shortly after dawn. The mine owner, however, apparently wasn't such an early bird.

Hank sat on a bench outside Mr. Hardt's office to wait, and Bear took his usual position next to Hank. "So what do you think Mr. Hardt wants to talk about?" He stroked the dog's head. "I know! I'll bet the mayor wants to congratulate you on your debut."

After the talent show—which they'd won, to Hank's astonishment—Mr. Hardt had introduced him to Ophelia Rathbone, and to a man named Clint Jones, who seemed to have taken an immediate dislike to him. After an awkward conversation, Hank had excused himself. Despite bad vision, he could see the situation clearly enough.

"Miss Ophelia Rathbone will soon be Mrs. Jones, if my guess is right. Can't say I'm that disappointed." Bear nudged

Hank's hand when he stopped petting. "You aren't disappointed either, are you?"

More likely, Mr. Hardt had called him here to tell him he was out of consideration. Should he accept the loss, or redouble his efforts to meet the requirements? He wanted the investment *and* Jolie, but it seemed he couldn't have both. As it was, she'd taken the decision away from him anyway.

Or had she?

Hank continued to rub Bear's ears. "Maybe you were trying to tell me something."

She'd come to the saloon to watch the talent show, or so she said, but she hadn't come inside. She'd been lurking at the periphery, peering in, yet holding herself at a distance. Bear had brought her inside and delivered her to him.

She could've run off, and Bear wouldn't have stopped her. The decision to stay must've been difficult for her, dealing with all the stares and whispers. Jolie acted tough, but Hank was sure she could be wounded by the insensitive comments people were bound to make. Still, she had bravely come up on stage and helped him salvage his flagging performance.

"I'm an idiot."

The dog rested his muzzle on Hank's knee.

"You're right, I should go talk to her. The way things are going I won't even get in on this investment. But you know what? Liam bought all the cards I offered to him, and he's already placed a big order for next year. It won't be enough to move out here, but Jolie could come back to Kansas City with us. How does that sound?"

Bear only sighed, but Hank knew he'd like having Jolie around.

Hank mulled over how his sister would react. If he

brought Jolie home as his wife, Maggie would welcome her with open arms. She'd told him repeatedly he needed to find someone he could love—and who would love him in return. If he offered Jolie his heart, she might open hers.

"Wonder what time it is?" he muttered.

Heavy steps echoed on the boardwalk, coming closer to where he sat. The shapes were large, and looked like two men. Was one of them Mr. Hardt?

A growl started in Bear's throat.

Hank straightened. His dog didn't growl unless...

"Looky here, Ned. It's that blind fella with his *friendly* little dog."

Hank clenched his fists on his knees. It was the miner who'd shot Bear and threatened Jolie, and he'd brought along one of his henchmen. Whatever the bully intended, Hank would be ready. Taking a cue from Jolie, he had tucked a derringer away where he could easily reach it inside his coat pocket. He hadn't fired a gun for seven years. What good was it to a man who couldn't see clearly enough to aim it? But he'd decided to pack one in case of extreme danger. This moment might just be considered extreme.

"Better not get too close, Bud. The beast might attack." Ned remained at a distance, which didn't give Hank much comfort. Fearful men were unpredictable, and could be every bit as dangerous as braggarts.

"If he comes at me, I'll have a good reason to put down the cur like I shoulda done before. That dog's a menace."

If Bud had intended to shoot Bear without provocation, he would've already done so. The bully was taunting them. Hank had dealt with bullies enough to know, the only way to defeat them, was to stand up to them without giving them the reaction they wanted.

"A menace? Bear?" Hank stroked the dog's head and

Bear quieted. "Darn near everyone in town has petted him, and he's made lots of friends. He even won the talent show. No one else we've met considers him a menace. Why don't we ask Charlie what he thinks? He told me yesterday he'd like to have a puppy sired by Bear."

Hank let the remark sink in. He made the point he knew the mine owner personally, and that Hardt liked his dog well enough to want its offspring, which was partly true. Charlie had remarked about the fine qualities Bear might pass on to a litter, and Hank had filed away the thought that the mayor would be first on the list for a puppy.

"Listen up, you blind bastard. I'm only givin' you one more warning. Leave town and don't come back. We don't want your kind here."

"I'm not sure Sheriff Draven agrees with you, but I'll consult with him on it. Oh, and by the way, he was here earlier, looking for both of you."

It was true Hank had seen the sheriff bright and early, and Draven had asked whether these men had caused more trouble. Now Hank could report back in the affirmative.

"Shee-it. Let's get out of here, Bud."

"Draven don't scare me."

So Ned was the more intelligent of the two.

Bear's growling got louder as Bud's shadowy form loomed.

"You're gonna regret goin' to the sheriff."

Hank slid his hand into his coat. He noted he was shaking as his fingers curled around the compact gun. "I don't think so."

Valentine's Day morning, Jolie rolled over in bed, pulled the pillow over her head and groaned. What was all that noise? Sounded like glass breaking. For once, when she tried to sleep in, one of the others had decided to get up early and have a party. After she'd locked up last night, as usual the last to seek her rest, she couldn't sleep.

She had to stop thinking about Hank. He wasn't destined to be part of her life. But if the other women wanted to find husbands, she wouldn't stand in their way. She'd mention this new mission to them and let them decide what they wanted to do. As for her, she had to be realistic about her own future. With brides rolling in, and those other crusaders eager to rid Noelle of vice, it was only a matter of time before she'd be run out of town. She might as well start packing.

With an annoyed huff, she threw off the covers and rubbed at the gooseflesh on her arms. She dressed in a hurry, choosing the warm wool over the thin silk. Later, once the house had warmed up, she could dress for business. Right now, the stoves needed be stoked and breakfast started. She couldn't wait until Milly returned. If Angelique had gotten up first, she would do it. Felice, no. Belle...maybe.

Jolie sniffed. Something was burning. *Ugh.* Had one of the girls tried her hand at cooking, then left food on the stovetop and wandered off? If she weren't around to correct this sort of mistake, they'd burn the place to the ground.

She flipped the long braid over her shoulder and threw open the door.

Smoke. Whitish gray, hovering. It slithered up from the stairs and undulated along the ceiling. Dread clamped a cold hand around her spine.

"Fire!" she screamed, racing down the stairs. In the

parlor, flames engulfed the curtains and the furniture, and were crawling up the papered walls. Smoke gyrated from the tips of the flames up to the ceiling. Broken glass lay on the floor, and she caught the distinct odor of kerosene. Had someone knocked over the lamp?

"Angelique! Felice! Belle!" Jolie yelled their names. Her lungs seized in the smoky air and she coughed. No one answered from the kitchen or back parlor.

The fire licked at the doorway into the hall, making the wood crackle, and the flames inched toward the balusters.

Oh dear God, it was spreading so fast.

She had to rouse the girls and get them down the stairs and out of the house before the fire and smoke blocked their way. Whirling around, still barefooted, she raced up the steps, screaming. "Wake up! The house is on fire!"

After the bully had stomped off, Hank breathed a sigh of relief. He couldn't see whether Bud had drawn on him, and without knowing for certain, he wouldn't have pulled his gun. As much as he despised men like Nance, the thought of killing a person made Hank's stomach turn. He'd once committed to saving lives, not taking them.

He leaned against the wall and after a moment, tapped his foot. How much time had passed? Maybe a half hour since those men had left. Mr. Hardt must've forgotten about the meeting. Regardless, Hank couldn't wait any longer. He had to let the sheriff know those two men might be plotting to ambush him, or worse, make trouble for Jolie.

With Bear in the lead, he started down the sidewalk toward the sheriff's office, which was at the end the block where the road veered off. It was quiet, still too early and cold for most folks to be out.

Hank pulled up the collar of his overcoat and adjusted the wool scarf to cover the lower part of his face. Up this high in the mountains, it was still the dead of winter and would be for some weeks to come. He still liked Noelle, despite the weather. The growing population was friendly, mostly, and it brimmed with opportunity.

Suddenly, Bear seemed eager to get going. As they drew closer to the corner, the dog began to pull. Hard.

"Stop. Why are you pulling me into the street? You know better than that."

Bear wouldn't stop even with Hank resisting, and he decided to go along, trusting the dog knew something he didn't. Fairly well-oriented, he realized they were headed in the direction of *La Maison*.

"Oh boy, not again. I didn't mean we'd go talk to her this early. If we wake her, she'll dump a chamber pot on our heads."

In the bright morning light, Hank could make out the now-familiar shape of the house. Mingled with the scent of the wintery mix squishing beneath his boots, was a faint smoky smell. Everyone had fires burning in this cold, but he hadn't notice the smell so strongly before. He slowed the dog down and found one of the hitching posts.

A loud bang startled him. Someone came stumbling out of the house, running toward him, and his heart sped up.

"Help! Help us! The house is on fire!" The woman threw her arms around his neck. He knew who the voice belonged to, Felice, but he couldn't smell her strong perfume over the stench of smoke.

He peeled Felice's plump arms from around his neck. "Where's Jolie?" he demanded.

"Still inside. She told me to run and get help, and she went after Belle and Angelique. Oh my God, it's burning down! It's going to burn down on top of them!" Felice wailed.

"How bad is it inside? Has the fire spread? Are the stairs clear?"

"I-I don't know. Jolie woke me and said the house was on fire. By the time I got out of my room, the smoke was already upstairs."

A fire like that would get out of control fast. They couldn't afford to wait for help.

Hank clamped down on a rush of fear. He stripped off his overcoat and gave it to Felice. The poor woman had to be freezing. "Go to the diner. Tell them people are inside, and we need a water brigade."

Felice dashed off.

Hank groped and found the metal ring on the hitching post. He tied the leash tight and checked the harness that ran beneath the dog's legs and around his shoulders to make sure it would hold. Bear couldn't help him in all that smoke. If he succumbed, he didn't want the dog to die too.

He hung his hat on the post, gave his best friend a hug, stood and said in a firm voice: "Stay!"

CHAPTER 12

*B*elle shrieked as Jolie dragged her out of the bedroom. "I'm in my nightgown!" That was one word for the sheer material draped over her body. "I'll freeze!"

"You'll burn up if you don't get the hell out of here!" Jolie yelled. She shoved the stupid girl toward the stairs. "Some chivalrous fellow will lend you his coat. Now get out of here!"

Dear God.

She had to remain calm. If she released the panic welling up inside and started screaming too, the girls might freeze up or do something odd in their terror. That had happened the last time she'd been in a burning building. A poor woman had perished trying to hide under the bed!

Belle held her hands over her nose. "I can't breathe. I can't see anything. There's too much smoke."

Jolie crouched low where the air was clearer. "Get down, close to the ground. There's air down here."

Belle dropped to her hands and knees and crawled toward the stairs.

Jolie tried Angelique's doorknob, but she'd locked it. "Angelique, wake up! The house is on fire, we have to get out!"

Why wasn't Angelique opening the door?

Jolie's eyes burned and tears streamed down her face, mostly from the stinging smoke, but also from fear. She kept seeing the charred body of that other woman with her mind's eye. "Don't be afraid, honey," she wheedled. "I'll get you out of here. Just please, open the door."

"Jolie!"

She jerked her attention toward the stairs, shocked at hearing Hank's voice. "Hank?"

He emerged from the stairwell and crawled toward her. "One of the girls ran past me. Where are you?"

"What the hell are you *doing* in here?"

"Rescuing you."

She reached out, grabbed his hand and pulled him to her, then gave him a hard hug, before she reared back and hit him on the shoulder with the flat of her hand. "Stupid damn fool!"

"You're welcome," he said, in between coughing. "Now let's get out of here. You can beat me later."

"I won't leave without Angelique. She's locked herself in her room."

"Show me."

Jolie put Hank's hand on the door. "Here."

Hank stood up, landed a hard kick, and the doorframe splintered. He kicked twice more until the door gave way, and Jolie rushed inside.

In the far corner, Angelique had crouched into a ball. She had her arms crossed over her head, protectively, and didn't seem to be aware of them.

Jolie grasped her arm and spoke quietly, but firmly,

"Angelique, honey, the house is burning down. We need to leave. Now."

Angelique drew away from her and pulled herself into a tighter ball.

"If she won't walk out, I'll carry her," Hank offered.

There was no time to waste talking to the terrified girl. Smoke was fast filling up the room, and for all they knew, the stairs were now on fire.

"All right. Hank's going to carry you." She scooped beneath Angelique's arms and lifted her so Hank could get a grip on her, but Angelique fought to get away.

Hank grabbed the girl, slung her over his shoulder, and took a firm hold across the back of her legs. "I have her. Show me the way out."

In the hall, the smoke was so thick, Jolie couldn't see. She also couldn't breathe standing up, and Hank was coughing behind her. She dropped to her knees and pulled at him. As soon he knelt beside her, Angelique broke free and wriggled away, heading in the wrong direction. Hank snaked an arm around her middle. "Oh no you don't," he rasped. "This is the way out."

Jolie crawled to the stairs with Hank following, dragging Angelique, whose loud keening raised the hair on Jolie's neck. When they started down the steps, he put Angelique in front of him. Jolie grasped her ankles, and together they coaxed and hauled her down the stairs. Flames had engulfed the wall next to the parlor. The heat was so intense she feared her clothes would melt. At last, they reached the bottom step, and she and Hank dragged a hysterical Angelique outside. Once there, an even worse noise could be heard, and it wasn't coming from Angelique. Bear's anguished howling continued until Hank went over to calm the poor dog.

Jolie swallowed, and her throat burned at the effort. She felt as if she'd been roasted in an oven. Another few minutes, and she would've been. Hank hadn't waited for help to arrive; he'd stormed into the house and braved the fire. The fact he'd left his dog outside meant he hadn't been very sure he'd make it back out. Jolie trembled. From cold or shock, she wasn't sure, but whatever it was, she couldn't make it stop.

Angelique had become compliant at last, but she still had that scary, blank look on her face. What had happened in there couldn't be blamed solely on her reaction to the current fire. Something else, something from her past, must have triggered her response. Whatever it was, it must've been horrible.

Jolie gathered her friend in her arms and began to rock her back and forth. "It's all right. We're safe. Hank rescued us."

"May I help?"

Jolie turned at the question. Holding out a blanket was the doctor's wife, the young woman Jolie had once teased so mercilessly. There was no censure or ill will in Cara's emerald green eyes, only kindness and mercy.

Angelique hung her head, her hair falling into her face, as Cara wrapped the blanket around her.

"She's..." Jolie tried and failed to come up with a word to describe her friend's terrifying state. "She locked herself in and wouldn't let me in her room. Hank kicked the door down, but she fought us, like she was afraid to leave."

"We'll take good care of her." Doc Deane picked up Angelique and carried her to a wagon. Colin was a good doctor, one of the best. If anyone could help Angelique, he could.

Now, for the first time, Jolie took in the crowd gathered

in front of the burning building. Men had lined up and were passing buckets of water, even snow. Women came running; some to look on curiously, but others joined the men in their efforts to put out the flames engulfing the house. The smoke grew darker, thicker, as it billowed out of a broken front window and from the open door.

Jolie stared at the awful sight with numb disbelief. *La Maison* was going to burn to the ground, and there was nothing she, or anyone else, could do about it. She expected anguish, grief, even rage. Her home would be gone in a matter of minutes, and so would her security.

The do-gooders had won. God had rightly smote the sinners, as her mother would've said. On the other hand, no one had died. Maybe God wasn't through with them, after all.

An ache in her chest joined the burning sensation in her throat. She rubbed her stinging eyes and turned away so she wouldn't have to watch her future crumble to ash. She had no choice now except to start over.

Over by the hitching post, Hank had retrieved his hat and had a hold of Bear's leash. He'd been speaking to the sheriff, and now he looked this way and that, as if he were searching for something or someone. She knew without a doubt he was looking for her. He'd never be able to see well enough to find her. Yet, he'd gone into that burning building to rescue her. Hank might've died...for her.

Emotion swept through her in a wave so strong, it made her breath catch and her knees tremble. If she mattered that much to him, she was worth more than she thought.

She wiped her nose with her sleeve and forced her numb feet through the snow, dragging her skirts as she walked up to him. With a sigh, she slipped her arms around his waist. On one hand, she wanted to strangle the idiot. Mostly, she longed to hold him tight and never let go.

"Good Lord, you're freezing. You need a coat." He gave her a hug then stripped off his suit coat and wrapped it around her.

Odd, she hadn't noticed the cold until he'd said something. "Why don't you have on an overcoat?"

"I gave it to Felice."

She glanced down at her red toes. "Do you happen to have an extra pair of shoes?"

Hank swept her into his arms. "Direct me to the store and we'll get whatever you need."

Jolie tightened her arms around his neck. All she really needed, she had right here. Suddenly, she recalled another treasure. "My Valentine card!"

Hank nuzzled her hair. "I'll make you all the Valentine cards you want."

She released a soft laugh, imagining the mess he'd make with paper and glue. Funny how she was more distressed about that card than about the money she kept locked up. If she couldn't recover the gold in the strongbox, she would be, quite literally penniless, and right back to where she'd started.

She ran her fingers over a smudge on Hank's cheek. "Promise me something."

"Anything."

"Promise you will never run into a burning building again."

His lips twisted into a wry smile. "I will, if you promise me you'll never be inside a burning building again."

She hugged him and buried her face against his neck. "I don't deserve you."

He kissed her on the head. "No, you don't deserve to be saddled with me, but that's what you're going to get, so you might as well prepare yourself."

CHAPTER 13

*H*owever long it had taken to build *La Maison*, it took far less time for the place to burn down. Jolie didn't stay to watch. As promised, Hank carried her over to the general store, while she directed him and Bear padded alongside. She peered over Hank's shoulder and saw Felice, still wrapped in his overcoat, and Belle, who someone else had taken pity on and given her a cloak. The two women trailed behind like forlorn baby geese.

When they got to Cobb's Pen, Avis opened the door, and with a solemn expression, watched them file inside. "Liam is helping the others. He opened the store so they could get buckets. Get whatever clothes you need, I'll find something for you to eat."

Hank insisted on purchasing Jolie new stockings and shoes, along with a new dress to replace the scorched one she'd been wearing, and a new coat, as well as necessary items she might need. Avis contributed the same for the other girls, and kindly offered them all a place to stay for the time being. Jolie couldn't make herself let go of Hank's arm.

The thought of leaving him made her feel panicked and sick to her stomach.

"You can stay with me," Hank told her.

"Whatever you want." Jolie said, and meant it. She would be at his beck and call for as long as he wanted her. If he decided he needed to become respectable and marry, she would remain available to him. She owed him her life.

She cradled his arm as she walked to the Golden Nugget, wearing her new shoes and carrying her other belongings in a large sack. Bear led with his tail wagging. Upon reuniting with his master, he'd showered Hank with affection as only a dog could.

They passed through the bar, which was eerily empty. Had everyone gone to watch *La Maison* burn? She noticed one of her flyers lying on the bar and remembered what the men who'd visited the night before had told them. There were more single men than married ones, and as long as this was true, *their girls* would have a place in this town.

Someone would rebuild, or they could run a business out of that abandoned house. Frankly, she didn't care. The only thing she could think about was how badly she wanted to be alone with Hank, so she could show him in every way she knew how that she'd be his girl, for as long as he wanted.

Her nerves jangled as she went with him up the stairs and into his room, knowing full well where this would lead. He undid Bear's leash and told the dog to go lay down. Ever obedient, Bear curled up on his blanket.

Jolie removed her coat, while Hank latched the door, then shrugged out of his coat and hooked his hat on a peg. Her hands shook as she worked on removing his tie.

When she began unbuttoning his shirt, he stopped her,

drew her hands to his lips, kissing her knuckles. "Is this why you think I brought you up here?"

She couldn't stop a smile. "I certainly hope so."

His lips curved slowly, sending shivers racing across her skin. "I'd like nothing better, but we'll have plenty of time later. You've been through hell, you need to rest for a little while, then get yourself prepared."

Leave it to Hank to do this his way. He'd made the point he wanted her to view him as being different from other men. She already did. Actually, he hadn't fit the mold from day one.

Jolie didn't resist when he drew her onto the bed, fully clothed, and cuddled her close. If he wanted to rest, she'd rest, so long as he held her. She desperately needed the *real affection* he'd offered before.

She snuggled against his shoulder and draped her arm across his chest. He toyed with her hair, which she'd long since given up worrying about. Long strands had escaped the braid she'd put it in the previous night. It was a bit difficult, considering her dress, to spoon herself against his warm, firm body, but she managed. She'd never liked to cuddle with other men. She'd not been able to enjoy sexual relations when it was a job. With Hank, it would be different. With him, *she* was different—softer, more vulnerable, but at the same time, stronger.

He took the end of a strand of her hair and tickled her cheek. *"Vous êtes mon amour et plus précieux que l'or."* His deep voice sent a thrill through her.

"What did you say?"

"I thought you knew French."

"No, I just picked the name *Jolie LaFemme* because I liked it. I learned later what it meant, and a few other choice French words. None of them polite."

His chest moved as he laughed. "I said, 'You are my love and more precious than gold.'"

Her heart stopped, as did her breathing.

My love.

Hank loved her, and he'd told her with the most beautiful words imaginable. If she lifted her head to look at him, she would burst into tears and start blubbering. She squeezed her arm around him and somehow managed to speak. "What are the French words for *I love you*?"

"*Je t'aime.*"

She swallowed until she'd regained her composure, then propped herself up on one arm. "*Je t'aime,* Hank Donovan... and I've decided to accept your offer."

"Have you now?"

"Indeed I have." She traced his lips as they curved into an adorable smile then kissed him, a long, lingering kiss, which left her aching for more.

Only, he didn't give her more. He nibbled a path to her ear, whispering, "Let's say our vows today. I can't imagine a more perfect day to get married than on Valentine's Day."

Vows?

Married?

Jolie drew back, more shocked than she'd ever been in her entire life. "You...you want to *marry* me?"

Hank's eyes crinkled with amusement. "What did you think I wanted?"

"A mistress."

His smile melted. He reached up and his fingertips traced her features, the touch sending tendrils of pure pleasure coiling through her. "No, sweet girl. I want to make you my *wife.* That's what *I* want. Is that what *you* want?"

He'd trained his gaze on her, and it seemed almost as if he could see her clearly. If so, he would know from the expression on her face there was nothing she wanted more, except for what she wanted for him.

Tears filled her eyes. "Marriage to me won't bring you respectability."

"The way I prefer to look at it, if you marry me, we'll both gain respect."

She began to cry in earnest. Wasn't it just like Hank to want to see in others the same goodness that was in his own heart? She would try to be more hopeful for his sake. But before he sacrificed so much for her, he deserved to know how little she had to offer him in return.

"I-I can't give you children. After I lost a child four years ago, I never conceived again. The doctor said it's likely I'm sterile."

Hank wiped her tears with his thumbs. "As long as we have each other, that's enough for me."

He kissed her again. She loved kissing him, touching him.

She ran her hands over his shirt. "Don't you want to take these clothes off?"

He drew her head down for another kiss. "We will," he said, in between kisses, "after we're married."

Jolie gazed at him in wonder. "You don't have to wait to prove you're different. I know you are."

Hank cupped her face in his hands. "This isn't about me proving anything. We're waiting because you're a lady, and I respect you."

"Oh, Hank." She wiped her face. "I don't deserve you."

"Stop saying that." This time he kissed away her tears. "This isn't about what either of us deserve. It's *love*, Jolie, pure and simple. Accept it."

Bear barked and ran to the door a moment before a light knock interrupted them.

"Mr. Donovan? Er, I hate to disturb yer rest."

"Seamus?" Hank gave Jolie a questioning look, and she shrugged. "What is it?"

"Mr. Hardt is lookin' for you. He wants ya to come to his office. Says it's...important."

Jolie felt Hank's jaw harden beneath her fingers, and the happy bubble he'd created around them burst. With this summons, he might be about to find out how much his love for her would cost.

Hank left Jolie in his room above the saloon to allow her privacy to freshen up before they wed. He asked Seamus if the barkeeper wouldn't mind finding the preacher, who wasn't in his room upstairs. In the meantime, Hank intended to give Charlie Hardt a piece of his mind.

He and Bear retraced their steps to the mining company's office, and when they entered, a chair scraped. Hank could make out that someone stood behind the desk.

"Have a seat, Hank. The chair is on your right."

Charlie Hardt might be the most influential man in town, but he wasn't Hank's boss.

"Thanks, but I'll stand. I don't intend to be here for very long. In fact, I almost didn't respond to your summons."

After a moment's hesitation, Hardt answered, "Summons? Is that how Seamus put it?"

The remark whipped Hank's annoyance into anger. "How else *would* he put it? He called me out of my room when I was...otherwise occupied." Hank would not drag Jolie through the mud by saying he'd been entertaining her in private, though it was likely Charlie, and everyone else, would assume the worst. "Frankly, I don't give a damn about your requirements. If I decide to invest in something, it will be on *my* terms, not someone else's."

"I see." The mayor moved around the desk.

Hank braced himself, wondering if the other man planned to punch him in the face for speaking his piece. He took a firm grip on the leash in case Bear started growling. He wouldn't sic his dog, but he wouldn't stand there and a take a thrashing either.

"Does that mean you're not getting married?" Hardt asked.

"No, I'm getting married...to Jolie," he added to make things perfectly clear. "Just as soon as we locate the preacher."

Hardt moved towards the front of the office where bright light indicated a window. He might be expecting someone else. That, or he was about to show Hank the door. "Chase went out to look at property for the parsonage, or he could be showing Ophelia and Clint home sites. They were married early this morning. That's why I was late."

"I'm not surprised or regretful to hear about Miss Rathbone's choice."

"No, I didn't expect you would be." As the mayor spoke, he returned to his desk, but didn't sit down. "I thought Draven might be coming back. He arrested one of the miners as a suspect; said you told him Bud started the fire."

"I wasn't eyewitness to the fact, but Mr. Nance made several threats a few days ago, and again this morning, which lead me to believe he might have done it. Also, Jolie said she'd seen glass on the floor of the parlor and smelled kerosene, and it looked like the front window had been broken."

"That sorry son of a bitch," the mayor swore. "He's been

E.E. BURKE

a troublemaker from day one. I should've fired him a long time ago."

"I hope it costs him more than his job," Hank said grimly.

The sound of the door banging open startled Hank.

"Hank?"

He turned to look behind him. "Jolie? What are you doing here?"

Bear's tail thwacked against Hank's leg as Jolie came up and took his arm. "I'm sorry, but the more I thought about it, I just couldn't sit around waiting. Not when you have so much at stake. Mr. Hardt, I beg you to reconsider."

A lump rose in Hank's throat. Jolie had come over here to plead on his behalf for something worth far less than her dignity. "Don't beg; it's not worth it. I already told him I'm not interested."

"From what I recall, we were discussing terms," Hardt replied.

Hank shook his head, confused. "We weren't negotiating. I told you what I thought about your requirements."

"Oh, I'm clear on that. Though I would like to know the basis for your objection."

He wanted more of an explanation?

"If you're open to hearing the truth, then I'll oblige."

"Careful," Jolie warned under her breath.

Hank slipped his arm around her waist to anchor her to him, found her cheek and kissed her. She needed to believe she was worth more to him than an investment in a mine, so he would show her. "If my marriage to Jolie excludes me from consideration, Mr. Hardt, then you can go hang."

CHAPTER 14

$\mathcal{H}$ank had just told the most powerful man in Noelle to go hang!

Bear barked. Was he adding his opinion too?

Jolie couldn't believe Mr. Hardt's reaction...a wry smile. Did the mayor think it was a joke?

After Hank had so bravely defended her, she couldn't keep silent. "Mr. Hardt, before you do anything rash, let me share what I came here to say."

The mayor nodded.

"For the past four years, I've seen a steady stream of so-called upright men come through my door. For the most part, they're self-centered, dishonest, unfaithful creatures. Integrity is just a word they use when they want people to think they're better than others." Jolie slipped her arm around Hank's back so they were holding each other. He gripped her side, but he didn't interrupt, and just let her continue.

"Then I met Hank, a man of true integrity. He showed me kindness and understanding, compassion without pity. He demonstrated how we ought to care for each other and rely on each other, no matter what. His courage sent him into a burning building, with no thought for his own safety, in an attempt to rescue four women who might've died if not for his quick actions. I can't think of *any* man in town more deserving of a chance to become an investor in Noelle's silver mine."

The mayor's gaze shifted over her shoulder and his smile became softer.

"I do believe she has a point, Charlie."

Jolie turned at the melodious voice. Mrs. Hardt had slipped through the door in time to hear Jolie's impassioned speech.

Mr. Hardt circled the desk as his wife came to meet him, and the two exchanged an affectionate hug and kiss. Penny had always been beautiful, but when she'd first arrived, she had acted unsure. Now, she exuded confidence. Something had changed. Perhaps love had been the catalyst.

"Mr. Donovan, my wife, Penny. Miss LaFemme, I believe you two have met."

Penny's smile put a knot in Jolie's stomach. Oh yes, they'd met. Jolie hadn't been nice to Penny either back when the brides had taken over *La Maison*. Pearl had told her Mrs. Hardt wouldn't hold it against her. If Pearl was right, Mrs. Hardt was one of those angels Jolie hated to love.

"Don't let me interrupt anything," Penny said. "Go on with what you were about to say."

"Well, let's see. Where was I?" Mr. Hardt touched his finger to his lips as if he couldn't recall, the man renowned for his steel-trap memory.

"Jolie was singing my praises," Hank suggested in a dry tone. As he spoke, he moved his fingers, stroking her side, letting her know with a touch how much he appreciated her passionate testimony.

Penny took her husband's arm. "I think we should have the editor write up an article about Mr. Donovan's brave rescue. That was quite a feat."

"He deserves more than an article. Give him a reward," Jolie suggested.

Hank's hand squeezed her side. She'd gone too far.

"Excellent idea!" Penny liked it though.

"I don't need a reward," Hank stated firmly.

Jolie gaped at him. What was he *thinking?* She and Penny were just about to convince Mr. Hardt to *gift* him the investment.

"Are you planning to settle in Noelle?" Being a smart man, Charlie Hardt quickly changed the subject.

Hank went back to stroking her side, attempting to soothe her ire. "That would be my plan. At present, I'm responsible for my sister's family, and I'd need to move them out here before I commit to anything."

"Yes, you need to be together," Jolie agreed.

"We *all* need to be together." Hank was reminding her she was now a part of his family.

The idea still seemed strange...and wonderful and miraculous.

Mr. Hardt's gaze turned speculative. "Liam Fulton told me you were looking for a place to open a business and hire women for a production line so you can produce more cards."

"That's an idea we've entertained. When we can afford it."

"Sounds to me like a good business for our town. One I'd like to invest in, if you're willing to consider it. The extra money might hasten your move out here."

Jolie's breath caught.

"Of course I'd consider it. That is..." A twinkle appeared

in Hank's eyes. "If you'll accept my investment in your business."

Jolie fought a smile. No wonder Hank had deflected the potential gift. He'd negotiated an even better deal for them.

Penny erupted into laughter. She clung to her husband's arm, smiling up at him. "Oh, Charlie, I do believe you've met your match."

Mr. Hardt didn't smile. However, his gaze conveyed admiration. "On your own terms, indeed. Very well, Donovan, it's a deal."

"Done." Hank put out his hand and Mr. Hardt grasped it. "We can work out the details later, after Jolie and I marry."

Mrs. Hardt walked over to the window. "Ah, I think I see Chase returning."

She went outside, snagged Reverend Hammond's arm and brought him into Mr. Hardt's office, along with his wife, Felicity, who appeared a little nervous. She might be recalling how Jolie had nearly bitten her head off.

"Mr. Donovan and Miss LaFemme would like to be married," Penny announced.

The preacher, looking a tad confused, nevertheless smiled. "Must be something in the air. I just performed another wedding this morning."

"Then you got plenty of practice," Mr. Hardt remarked. "Now marry these two, so Hank and I can work out our business deal."

Mrs. Hardt came to Jolie's side. "I'd be honored to stand with you."

"I'm honored you want to." Jolie glanced at Hank, who'd reached down and taken her hand, twining their fingers.

Of course, Hank's dog was his best man. Bear sat back on his haunches, looking very noble. Mr. Hardt stood behind Bear, acting as a second witness.

The preacher and his wife faced them, and Reverend Hammond opened his Bible.

Jolie's heart leapt into an all-out gallop.

"Dearly beloved..." Reverend Hammond's recitation droned on.

Dismay twisted the knot in her stomach. She hadn't been entirely truthful with Hank about what he might consider a very important fact. Somehow, it just never seemed to be the right time. *Face it.* She'd avoided telling him for fear he would laugh in her face.

"Hank Donovan, do you take Jolie LaFemme—"

"That's not the name I was given at birth," she blurted out. "If...if that makes any difference."

"It makes a difference if you wish to legally wed Mr. Donovan," Felicity pointed out.

Jolie gnawed her lip as the others waited. How embarrassing. "It's...Purity. Miss Purity Asgood."

Everyone stared at her, which helped fan the fire already burning her face.

Hank smiled slowly. At least he wasn't rolling on the floor, laughing. He turned his gaze on her, and even though she knew he couldn't make out her features, he saw her more clearly than anyone had ever seen her. "That's a good name for someone whose love is pure."

Jolie's eyes filled with tears. *Sweet man.* If anyone's love was pure, it was Hank's.

As other kind smiles appeared, her nerves stopped jangling, and a profound sense of peace came over her. They could all share a good laugh *after* the wedding. Then she would have them sign in blood not to reveal her given name outside of this room.

"Make it legal, preacher." Then she said to Hank. "Promise you'll call me Jolie."

He touched her face, lovingly. "To me, you'll always be Jolie. *Très Jolie.*"

The End

Want to read Mr. Hardt's story?
Check out *The Drum*

AUTHOR'S NOTE

The *Brides of Noelle* came about as a result of the wonderful reader response to our *Twelve Days of Christmas Mail-Order Brides* series, and features stories set in the same fictional town of Noelle, Colorado.

If you're wondering whether Bear is actually a "seeing-eye dog"... Well, not exactly. After World War I, a doctor in Germany noticed the protective behavior of his dog around patients and set up some experiments, but the first recorded training of seeing-eye dogs occurred in England. That's not to say there weren't blind people who discovered how smart dogs were long before that. Hank, being a very smart man, connects with Bear, a very smart dog, and the two learn from each other. Yes, I'm taking liberties by having Hank "train" Bear, but I don't think it's so far off to be unbelievable.

When I first conceived this story, I was a little concerned about featuring a prostitute as the heroine because I wasn't sure readers would be able to relate to her. Although this is technically a Sweet Romance, I didn't sanitize Jolie. I did try very hard to humanize her and explore emotions that any woman could understand and appreciate. I thought her story would be fascinating to research and write. Finding her perfect hero, now *that* was a challenge!

All the best,

E.E. Burke

ABOUT THE AUTHOR

E.E. Burke is a bestselling author of historical fiction and romances that combine her unique blend of wit and warmth. Her books have been nominated for numerous national and regional awards, including Booksellers' Best, National Readers' Choice and Kindle Best Book. She was also a finalist in the RWA's prestigious Golden Heart® contest. Over the years, she's been a disc jockey, a journalist and an advertising executive, before finally getting around to living the dream--writing stories readers can get lost in.

Find out more about her books at her website: www. eeburke.com.